Honor Among Vampires

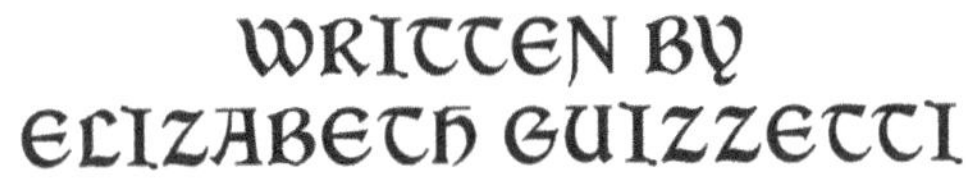

Edited by Joe Dacy
Cover and Interior Illustrations by Elizabeth Guizzetti

Printed in the United States of America

Paperback ISBN-13: 978-1-950708-06-2
Ebook ISBN-13: 978-1-950708-05-5

This book is dedicated to Dennis.
I would walk into eternity with you.

A Note From the Author:

"Agata, the eldest vampire in the Paper Flower Consortium, was a wise woman both in the ancient and current meaning of the words."
Death Pulls a Stake Out (A Norma's Cleaning Service Mystery #1)

SOMETIMES AUTHORS HAVE TO FOLLOW WHERE their muse leads.

As I've mentioned in the Foreword of *Death Pulls a Stake Out*, I never expected to write these stories, but my goal with The Paper Flower Consortium Universe is to keep them consistent, even if they are different genres. I knew by the type of story it was, *Honor Among Vampires* would be Gothic fiction. In contrast, *Immortal House* is a horror-comedy, *Norma's Cleaning Service Mysteries* are cozy mysteries with a vampire detective.

Unlike most of my work, I wrote this book in three separate fragments. The truth is with everything else regarding *Immortal House*; it started as a joke. I figured since Vlad Dracula was a Wallachian nobleman; Agata could be from Moldavia. They were neighbors joined by the Carpathians. I wrote a few scenes of back story for her and set them aside simply so I could write how she related to Laurence.

After *Immortal House*, I began writing the *Norma's Cleaning Service Mysteries*. Norma's relationship with the coven and its members are wholly different than Laurence's. As I grew to know the aspects of the vampires which Laurence didn't know (or bother to report) Agata's story resounded in my brain. I wrote a detailed outline of the significant historical facts and interactions of all the six elder vampires of the Paper Flower Consortium. This helped me decide how to build the coven in more detail. Between writing *Death Pulls a Stake Out* and *Death Hears a Siren*, I wrote *Honor Among Vampires*.

Agata's story takes place in the Principality of Moldavia. I researched Romanian vampire myths, the former and current culture, and Roman, Saxon, and Ottoman influences upon the Medieval Period. Using a historical map, I made up the county and town of Râuflor – though if it existed it would lie on the northwestern part of historical Trotus. By its description, the county lies in the Carpathians and needed to be close to ancient and 16th-century roads.

The title page illustration has a traditional pattern from Romania minus the bats. The two title illustrations are both cultural symbols of Romanian spring and harvest festivities and physical items that would be close to Agata's heart. Mărţişors are a symbol of spring. Traditionally women collect herbs before the fall equinox. The final drawing was inspired by the painting *La Belle Dame Sans Merci* by Sir Frank Dicksee.

I want to thank Joe Dacy, who edited this book. I also want to thank my author buddies: N.D. Fessenden beta-read it and did a final proofread, Ashleigh Gauch listened to my fears about this storyline, and Jennifer Brozek chatted with me about the premise of a multi-genre series. And thanks to my husband, Dennis, who has supported me in all my writing.

I hope you enjoy it!

Moldavia
Spring 1509

Chapter 1

AGATA ARTURESCU VIDRARU COMPOSED A letter to her husband as she watched two of her five children outside her kitchen window. A great tactician, Jakub Petruescu Christian, had fought in several battles. In the seventeen years of their marriage, Jakub had been gone for nine in separate actions. It had been almost four years since he last graced their home. Worse, Agata hadn't received a letter from him in seven months. She prayed each night, but that did not stop her fear of plague which afflicted the army. Their current Voivode was troubled by never-ending invading forces of the Ottomans, Polish, Wallachian, among others and broken alliances with those countries just as his father had been.

Before her disquiet got the better of her, Agata reminded herself, "Snow came early last year; the new spring had just arrived. Jakub's fine. It's hard for letters to cross the mountains during the winter. One day, several letters arrive. If God is kind, my husband will deliver them himself."

Outside, Artur untied Daciana's Mărţişor from her tunic. A powerful talisman, the twisted white and red string ended in two tassels and held a silver charm. It seemed so universal. Red: the color of fire, blood, darkness, death, passion, and women. White: the color of ice, air, light, life, wisdom, and men.

"Tie it high this year!" Daciana demanded. "I don't

want the goat to get it!"

Agata wrote how proud Jakub would be of their elder son. Artur, a lad of fourteen, who, over the past winter, had grown as tall as Agata. His voice lowered. He lived in the bachelor's quarters and wore a short sword and dagger on his belt. He had employment in the service of Jakub's brother, Count Mihai. He took guard duty with the other men, but he also counted the cows for Agata, studied their family's accounts, and had never lost even the most reticent heifer. Most importantly to Agata, he never lost patience with his youngest sister, the only child still at home. Like all four-year-olds, Daciana could be both loving, selfish, and taxing—often all at once.

"Your wish is my command." Artur's sepia eyes, which he inherited from Agata, had a haunting focus on his little sister's errand. Any man would be proud to have such a son. His back was straight; his shirt and woolen coat hid his wiry muscles. He jumped onto a low branch. His dark hair was mussed; his tanned skin made ruddy by the spring wind blowing the fragrance of the mountains into the valley.

Halfway up the apple tree, he called: "This high? Next to Mothers?"

"No. As high as yours." Daciana jumped around the tree, her black hair flying in the wind.

Artur climbed two more branches and tied the red and white string beside his own. The tassels fluttered in the breeze.

Agata sighed. While she and the servants had also tied their Mărţişors to the tree, only Artur and Daciana would tie theirs to the apple tree this year.

Her eldest, Irina, now sixteen, had married the spice merchant's eldest son and made a fine house on Merchant Street. As part of the marriage contract, her younger son, Petru, had received an apprenticeship with the spice merchant. No doubt, they would tie their Mărțișors to a tree in the center of town. Her middle daughter was in the grave; Little Daniela had not lived long enough to see the turning of a single year.

"We'll be strong all year!" Daciana shouted.

Artur lowered himself; careful not to land on his sister.

"Let's play Old Blind Woman!" Daciana said.

"I've guard duty," he said, pointing at the sundial.

"You never have time to play with me anymore." She pouted and wrapped her arms around his leg. "And Mama has to make bread today. Please."

He rested his hand on her head. "If you promise to stay out from underfoot, you can tag along and be a soldier today."

"Mama, I'm a soldier," she yelled toward the kitchen window.

Agata waved. "Listen to your brother and the other men."

Smiling, she returned to her letter.

She wrote how she was teaching Daciana her alphabet. Their youngest spelled out merchant signs around their town and could write cat, cow, goat, and dog on a wax tablet.

The sundial showed it was noon when Daciana dashed into the kitchen, jumped up and down with her eternal energy. "Mama, Auntie's coming!"

She ran out again, the kitchen door slammed in its frame. Agata set her writing supplies high on a shelf, rang for Cook, and went to greet her sister-in-law. They had bread to bake.

The count's towered castle situated on the hill on the east side of Râuflor also had a bread oven, but they used Agata's kitchen. While Count Mihai never minded paying for the flour or wood, he hated the mess, Cook's songs, women's talk, and the laughter of the children who stole bits of dough.

Tomorrow, as they did every Saturday, Agata and Countess Gavrilla Musca Ricescu would pass loaves of bread to the peasant farmers, merchants, servants, soldiers, and priests as was their duty. Râuflor was not only the county seat and oversaw seven villages but was the largest town in the area. Many farmers and hunters made the trip to collect their bread and buy and sell wares at the large market day. If the day was profitable, they might purchase goods at the row of permanent stores.

Gaverilla's footman helped the countess off the wagon. Her servants unloaded the heavy bags of flour and carried them into the kitchen. Daciana bowed, then hugged the countess around her waist. Gavrilla picked her up and kissed her cheeks. She smoothed her linen le and fata once she set the child back on the ground. Daciana scampered back to Artur who was still on guard duty.

The women kissed each other on the cheeks.

Agata touched Gavrilla's plump belly carrying her fourth child. "And how is my little niece or nephew?"

"Kicking, but not as hard as my boys. It might be a girl this time," Gavrilla crossed herself. "I apologize for my lateness; Bogdan came to argue with my husband."

Agata had an icy feeling in her chest. She knew what Bogdan wanted. Though he shared a name with their Voidode, the parish priest's behavior was anything but princely. He had hinted Jakub had died in battle and Agata might consider a husband who was home.

However, she was no fool. Bogdan didn't have eyes for her. He desired her fine house and profitable dairy. Marrying his cousin's widow would be an honorable way to leave the priesthood which he complained about to Mihai when he thought others weren't listening. Moreover, he had despised Jakub since they were boys. Agata did not like to think her husband had bullied his common-born cousin, but Bodgan's eyes alighted with joy at the thought of Jakub's demise.

Her hands felt clammy. She struggled to open the crock of maia. Cook took the jar away from her. The smell of yeast filled the kitchen.

"He feels I should take suitors," Agata said in a flat voice.

"Yes." Gavrilla sat on a wooden bench. She measured the water and thinned the maia.

"My husband will come home," Agata said.

"Of course, Jakub will come home," Gavrilla said. "The count will not consider otherwise."

"Perhaps, you ought to look for a daughter-in-law." Cook weighed the litrăs of flour for the first batch in a long wooden bowl. "You have a grown son. When Artur takes a wife, there'll be more babies in the house."

"My son will marry after he finishes his education, Cook," Agata said, careful not to speak too harshly. One should never talk sharply when baking bread. It spoiled the rise.

"Move Irina and her man back into the house," Cook suggested and carefully measured the thinned maia into the flour.

Agata stirred it with a wooden spoon until a loose dough formed. She placed a damp linen rag over the bowl and set the dough aside.

"Oh, Cook, Irina enjoys being mistress of her own house." Gavrilla prepared more maia with water for the next batch. "Please, we must continue our toils before night. It is the seventh day after the full moon, and the count has made a fine sacrifice for the Legatus. A yearling hogget with the fluffiest pure white wool."

"Continued blessings for our wise count and beautiful countess," Cook said.

Like every count whose county surrounded the nearby Carpathians (whether or not they be Wallachian or Moldavian) Mihai would leave one perfect ewe in the field on the ancient calendar. Or at least, that was what Agata had been told. She had only been to two counties. The one she was born and the one into she married. During his life, her father also put out a sheep outside his township only it was the tenth night after the full moon. Nowadays, her younger brother bore the responsibility.

Though the counts paid their tributes and the peasants feared vampires, Agata didn't believe in the myths of the old Roman Legatus who lived in the crumbling Roman ruins on top of the highest mountain. She credited a family of brigands for using a well-told myth to keep themselves in relative comfort. Legends could be eternal. Like the old saying went: some things were more lasting than bronze.

"Too bad, we can't sacrifice a priest who refuses the vows of poverty and looks at other men's wives," Cook said.

"Why would a vampire want an irritable old priest?" Gavrilla said. "His meat probably tastes as dry as twenty-year-old ram!"

The women looked at each other and laughed. The sound of joy lightened Agata's spirits.

"A donia," Gavrilla said.

"As Countess wishes." Cook improvised a happy song to help Agata forget her troubles and bless Gavrilla's coming-child.

*

AGATA MOVED ABOUT HER HOME, PREPARING for the night. Her back was stiff from the long day's work. The smell of fresh bread followed every step as her soft leather shoes shuffled along her stone-tiled floor. Every step was lit with her candle.

Tomorrow, the sun would rise. However, tonight, the full moon was hidden by the deep clouds in the sky. Outside, the wind blew and rattled the leaded glass windows which she checked and latched one by one. No doubt, the servants would whisper their superstitious stories as they held each other in the night.

Even if she spent all night in prayer, she would pine for Jakub. She hoped he was alive, but feared her husband was dead. At thirty-two, Agata was still young enough to have a few more children if God would bring Jakub home.

She checked the nursery, which seemed eerily quiet. Only, Daciana still nestled in her nurse's arms. The two were burrowed under a wool blanket and a heavy cow skin. The windows were already locked tight. In silence, Agata padded out of the nursery.

The manservant, Florin, bowed his head. "The kitchen and buttery are locked up for the night, my lady, but your son is calling."

"Thank you."

Agata hurried down the stairs into the hall where Artur waited.

"Lady Mother, one of the first-year heifers suffers from calving—Robert requested your guidance."

"Yes, my son. I'm coming." Though her back ached, she was grateful for the distraction. As it had been a day full of heavy work, she was mostly dressed for such a venture. She removed her embroidered slippers and put on heavy boots. She pulled a cloak over her everyday cotton le and woolen fata. Her maramă, which covered her coiled black hair, was plain linen.

The manservant's hand trembled on the open door. "My lady, it is late. Be wary of the Legatus."

"I've my son to protect me, and the count put out a

perfect sacrifice. Keep the house locked uptight," Agata said.

He inclined his head at her.

As the younger daughter of a Count and the wife of a Count's younger son, Agata couldn't be too safe when it came to money. Who knew when Jakub would return? Her own mother died in poverty, because of the taxes and tithings-owed after Agata's father and elder brother died. With Jakub's blessing, Agata became a learned midwife and kept a profitable dairy. She couldn't afford to lose a cow and her calf. The cows were her children's inheritance. Artur and Petru were coming to the age where she would need to negotiate marriage—even if they didn't marry right away. She hoped Jakub would be home when that happened, but she knew his wishes on the matter.

Artur held her arm; Agata shivered in the cold air. They crossed the narrow path through the herb garden where soft leaves brushed against her skirts as if to protect her from adventuring into the night. The wind changed, and Agata inhaled the perfume of her everlasting rosemary. Her other herbs and peppers had not bloomed yet.

With the great house behind her, Agata's eyes adjusted the darkness as they picked their way across the meadow to the birthing barn. Her herdsman, Robert Robescue, waited for them.

The cow wrung her tail and tried to kick her stomach. She snorted and mooed weakly yet seemed restless.

"Shh, how's my good girl. I'll help you. Let us give her a bit of fresh hay. How long has she been in labor?" Agata asked.

"She wasn't in labor after midmeal, but didn't want to come in from the pasture tonight, Lady," the herdsman said.

Agata removed her cloak, rolled up her sleeves, and washed her hands with cold water and potash soap. She rubbed pressed oil onto her hands and arms.

She used more oil to feel the cow's cervix. She observed the calf's head and a frothy mouth and nostrils, but no hooves. The calf was straight on rather than leaning to its right, worse, the cow's water had broken.

"She is dilated, the head is in the birth canal," Agata said.

"Will we lose her, Lady Mother?" Artur asked.

"She just needs a little help."

"Walk slow, Artur," Robert said. "New mothers can be skittery."

Agata reoiled her arm and waited for the next contraction. Once it passed, she pushed the calf into the correct position. She sang a donia to the cow and prayed. Another contraction, then another.

Two hours later, she had a healthy mother and baby.

"Robert?" Agata called. No response. "Artur?" She peeked out of the stall. The men's frames leaned against the far wall asleep, next to several buckets of water and a bar of soap.

She thought about waking them, but instead, she washed the cow as the new mother licked her baby clean. Wet, but happy in her night's good work, she stole a moment to gaze upon her angelic son. She wouldn't embarrass him by treating him like a boy in front of another man, but she felt a deep sadness that she would never embrace him like a boy again.

Outside, there was a low howl. A chicken squawked from the coop. The cows in the main barn mooed in protest and fear.

"It is just an animal," Agata said, but still felt the need to cross herself.

She decided once she was back inside, she would sleep in the nursery with Daciana tonight.

Agata whispered a prayer. "Dear God, please return

my husband to me. I miss him so much."

The priests said the most important thing a noblewoman could do was bear children for her husband and to produce knights for the Voivode's army which protected their country from generations of invaders. It was her duty and honor. So she added to the prayer. "If he returns, I'm still young enough to give him another child or two. Bless me with more children."

She shook Artur awake.

"What is it?" He asked, rubbing his eyes.

"A girl calf, my son. We've been fortunate tonight."

"And the mother?" Robert yawned.

"Both are doing well." Agata said, "It's late. Artur, did you plan on sleeping in the house tonight or going back to the bachelor's quarters? Robert, I can put you with the servants if you don't want to cross town under the darkness."

Another howl interrupted her words. This one sounded closer. Wolves never came in this close to the walled city. She thought she heard a horse. *Jakub.*

Robert jumped to his feet. "Stay here, my lady."

He was just out of sight when he bellowed. The door to the birthing barn slammed shut.

"What is it?" Artur called.

Robert shouted. Another voice added to the deafening noise. Moos became brays of panic. Something hard hit the barn door. The door rattled. The entire barn trembled. She held her cross tightly and said a prayer under her breath.

Artur grabbed Agata's wrist and pulled her behind him. He drew his short sword.

The wooden door cracked. A board was ripped off the door. A massive arm silhouetted against the night sky. Another board broke.

"Who's there? I am armed," Artur warned.

The only answer was the door being ripped away.

An unseen force of wind and movement kicked up the hay. Agata could only see a huge black mass as she was thrown away from Artur. She screamed her son's name as a battle cry filled the air. Artur shouted in return. There was a short clanging of metal. Then the sound of something fleshy hitting the barn wall, or perhaps a stall door.

Darkness was all around her.

"God, help us!"

The cow bleated in panic; the calf squealed. Hay rose in the sky as the cow kicked and bucked.

Hands clamped on Agata's shoulders.

She was pushed against the wall. Her maramă was ripped from her head. Hands pulled her plaited, coiled hair. She screamed as two piercing blades ripped into her throat. She slapped, scratched, and kicked her attacker, but he only buried the blades deeper.

She couldn't see her son, only blackness. "Artur, Artur!"

"By rights, you're mine," a low husky voice whispered.

Agata felt as if she was being smothered by darkness. Her mind grew wooly, and her arms fell to her sides. Weakened, she couldn't breathe. She thought her heart would explode. She fell into darkness.

*

Chapter 2

AGATA AWOKE AGAINST THE WALL OF THE BARN, Florin and Cook stood over her. Their faces set in concern. Her skirt and shirt were covered in sticky blood and birthing liquid. She touched her bare head; her hair had been freed. A strange man had seen her hair. The fiend had touched it. Her throat and tongue were swollen with thirst. Her skirts were ripped. Her body felt torn. She must do nothing to expose her injuries, until she was sure.

"Cia?" she croaked.

"In the house, my lady." Cook found her maramă and handed it to her.

"My baby girl, my God, was she touched?" Agata covered her head.

"No, my lady. We were tucked safe in our bed until this morning when the household staff realized you were still in the barn."

Artur. A cold feeling spread through her heart. "Artur? My son?"

"I don't see him," Florin said.

"Artur," she called.

He did not answer.

Though her throat felt like it was coated in dust, she called louder, "Artur!"

Using the wall and Cook as support, she rose to her feet. Her knees felt watery, but she stood as tall as she could.

In the birthing stall, her first-year heifer was on its side, breathing heavily. Shallow wounds covered her body. Beside her, the calf was crushed. She had lost a calf!

Agata licked her lips. Her throat ached, parched by dryness. Her tongue was cracked. Her mind screamed to press her lips to her sweet cow. If she could press her lips to her cow's wounds, the blood would banish this mad thirst.

Her mind flew to Saint Photina, the Samaritan woman who spoke to Jesus at the well. Photina suffered many tortures at the hand of the Emperor Nero for her faith, eventually being tossed down a well. Jesus had told the woman if she drank from the well, she would always be thirsty, but if she drank the water he gave her, she would never thirst. Agata was a woman of God, a follower of Christ, yet she felt as if she drank from a well of corruption and sin. Her thirst would never slacken.

"Artur? Artur!"

In a daze, Agata wandered the barn, clutching Cook's arm. They found his sword on the ground. She discovered her son, lying on his back in another stall, against the far wall, half-buried in dirty hay. Bleeding from a wound on his arm and a gash across his brow.

"Artur!" She screamed. He did not move. She pressed her ear on his chest. He was breathing. His fingers on his right hand were broken, and he had a lump on his head. She pulled her son to her chest and rocked him tightly. "My boy, my angel."

Artur's eyes fluttered open. "Ma, Mother? I wasn't able to stop them. I'm sorry."

Sobbing in relief, she said, "We're alive. We'll send a messenger to the magistrate. Where's Robert?"

"My lady, don't grieve, but your herdsman is dead," Cook said. "Outside. His throat has been ripped out."

Agata sobbed harder. With his uninjured hand, Artur helped her to her feet. His eyes full of tears which did not fall. "I'll wait for the mayor, you're overwrought." He lowered his voice, trying to sound like a man.

Agata told him. "I might need to defend my honor."

Artur straightened. He was his mother's son, but that did not give her comfort. "Mother! What does a woman know about anything? With my father in the world, I speak for this house."

"Yes, my son," she said. "Forgive me."

"There is nothing to forgive, you're overwrought. Take my mother to her woman," Artur ordered the servants.

What am I to tell Jakub? Would he believe me? Divorce was legal, but Jakub's family wouldn't suffer the loss of the family's honor. However, at this moment, Agata was the mistress of her house. She found her voice again. "And Florin will bring you a fresh cămaşa, pieptar and bandages to splint your fingers. You're covered in filth, my son."

He thanked her.

Agata held Cook's arm. She told herself not to look at the body. Yet when they passed Robert, his eyes stared at the endless sky and his throat was covered in dried blood.

While Artur awaited for the mayor, Agata called for water and went into her private chamber. Every wall was covered with thick tapestries of flowers, leaves, unicorns and symbols of astronomical power from several countries, proof of Jakub's devotion to her and the children.

Her arms were covered in scratches, and her body was torn by whatever the brute did to her. She had several bite marks, punctured pairs of small wounds. She tried to remember, but it had been so dark.

Dear God, please, let me not be pregnant.

If she was pregnant and Jakub was not here, her in-laws might accuse her of being an adulteress. Jakub's brother, Count Mihai, hated scandal above all. Perhaps she should provide betrothals for her younger children, especially Daciana, before her loss of honor was discovered.

She jumped at a knock on the door and covered her body with her sleeping coat. Her maid, Elana, came in with two buckets of steaming water which she poured into the tub. She sprinkled in rose petals.

"Are you badly injured?"

"I don't know." Tears crested her eyes and dripped down her cheeks. "I'm so sorry for Robert's death, yet so happy Artur lived. I feared he was dead too."

"As any mother would," Elana said. "Forgive me, but the guards want to know about the bread?"

She remembered the day. She was a lady of the county. People depended upon her.

"We'll distribute the bread as planned, but I must bathe," Agata said.

"As you wish, my lady," Elana said.

Agata wondered what her maid suspected, what her whole house suspected.

Another servant brought in two more buckets. Her maid brought the final two. Agata touched the water. It was uncomfortably hot, but she climbed inside. The maid washed her face, her body, then left her to soak.

Knowing she only had minutes before the maid returned, she left the tub with a cup of soapy bathwater and opened her box of herbs. She seeped several bitter buttons.

Through the walls, she heard Daciana playing (and disobeying to her nurse) who was trying to dress her appropriately. With her elder brothers and sister grown, she was often a lonely child with only adults for company.

Agata drank from the potion. She held down the sharp-smelling, soapy water as long as she could. She vomited in her chamber pot, prayed, and sobbed in silence.

She dressed in embroidered flax for the day, careful to ensure her costume was in order and proclaimed her station and her husband's great love. Her neck was covered in a high collar, a string of beads, and a Holy Cross. She combed and braided her hair and wrapped it in a snood. Agata carefully placed her veil and embroidered maramă. She covered her bruised hands with gloves.

Uninvited, male voices invaded her chamber from the window. Her fists squeezed the cold iron shutters as she spotted Artur and the manservant speaking to the magistrate and two deputies. The shutters were decoratively sculpted like leaves, but they felt like bars. Dishonored noblewomen were known to be walled into their homes, but she doubted Count Mihai would go to the expense. It would be cheaper to have her killed.

Trying to calm her nerves, she inhaled. The sweet and spicy perfume of her herb garden was absent. All she could smell was death. She gazed at the Mărţişors dangling from the apple tree; the tassels stirring in the wind. She must be strong for her children's sake.

Agata thought about calling down to the men, but she had a grown son to speak for her. He would decide to bring charges on behalf of his father — or not.

Their callous eyes stared up at her when they heard she was in the birthing barn. These were hard men. They knew the world. Even if Artur wouldn't say the words: they must know she was raped. Yet, no one spoke of it. Perhaps, it was because if Jakub was dead on a battlefield, her rapist wouldn't even be charged. Perhaps, if she was not pregnant, the silence was better than scandal.

After they left, Agata went to speak to Artur. "What did you tell them, my son?"

"We were attacked and robbed last night. We were both injured, but our poor herdsman was murdered. Some peasants whispered the Legatus came down from the mountain, but the magistrate told me our assailants will be caught and hung for murder."

Injured? Tears splashed her cheeks. She was so furious; she couldn't look at her son in the eyes. Her assailant would be hung for murder. *Stop weeping! What good would it be for the count's sister-in-law to be embroiled in a scandal?*

"I'm sorry that you lost a friend, my beloved son, I know how you felt about Robert. Would you help calm an old woman today?"

"Of course, Mother, you have nothing to be frightened about, not anymore." He kissed her left cheek and then her right.

Daciana ran to Artur. "Our Countess is coming! I'm passing bread to the peasants, I'm passing bread to the peasants."

Her brother knelt and gave her a kiss on the cheek. "Are you coming with the soldiers?" she asked.

"Your brother has business to conduct today with your uncle," Agata said. "Are you ready to go? Here comes your noble aunt."

Gavrilla and her entourage approached the house. How would she face her? She was her dearest friend and sister-by-law, but she was still a Countess and must protect the county above all. Gavrilla was too intelligent to not know something was wrong.

Agata trembled.

"Perhaps you ought to stay home, my mother?" Artur said.

With more confidence than she felt, she put her quaking hands on her hips and stated, "And set idle tongues on me? No, my son, that will not do. The peasants need their Sunday bread."

*

Chapter 3

AGATA WALKED BESIDE GAVRILLA ALONG THE fortified walls. Râuflor was the largest defended town in several counties, but today thick, stone walls provided no comfort. Several Guild towers were erected around the city by the Saxons to protect the town from the Turkish raids. The two soldiers walking in front of them seemed too young and inexperienced to offer protection. Daciana jumped, hopped, and skipped. She stopped to pluck a stray flower and handed it to Agata. Their servants and yoked oxen carried the baskets of bread. They passed the city gate carved with the words: GOD IS LOVE and several solar crosses below. Every fruit-bearing tree bore Mărțișors.

Two peasant women moved out of the countess's path. One held an infant, who Agata had delivered, snug at her breast.

Peasant farmers set up their wears for market day. As they did every Saturday, she and Gavrilla set the wagon in the town square in the shade of the tallest tower.

Statues of Romulus and Remus stood at the door of the tower, above them was a carving of the giant wolf who suckled them. The clocktower was topped with the family signet to symbolize the accountability of the Town Council to the count who in turn was accountable to the Voivode. Besides the towers sat the gallows and a set of stocks. A woman and man sat clamped in irons. The sign above their head said: THIEVES. They looked drawn and cold. *If the*

Legatus had come, wouldn't they be dead?

I don't believe in the Legatus! She shuddered as she felt the deadly reminder of men's cruelty. *How many of my midwife sisters lost their lives in this square hung as witches?* Agata had lost her honor. If Jakub wanted a divorce, the count would not tolerate the scandal. She would be killed. Not hung publicly in a square, her death would be discreet.

Mihai would give Jakub a new wife before Agata's body went cold. The carved wooden porch and iron shutters would protect someone else from the rain. The new wife would remove Agata's tapestries and insist on new ones. She would change the carpet. She might paint over the flowers and fertility symbols which Agata's hand-painted on the row of tiles under the roof. Agata would slowly be erased.

"Are you all right, my sister?"

She coughed. Her tongue weighed a thousand drams. "I'm thirsty, my dear Countess."

Gavrilla snapped her fingers. A young soldier brought Agata a leather of watered wine. The wine did not quench her thirst, but she thanked him.

The sun stung her eyes. She drew her veil over her face. She could not look at the men as she passed loaves to each family. She didn't know if one —or several— of them was Robert's murderer, Artur's assailant, her rapist.

Peasants whispered the Legatus of the Mountains had come down to feed on the populace last night. Several cows and pigs had gone missing. Artur and his mother were attacked. Robert was killed. She felt their eyes on her.

"What is it, dearest sister Agata?"

"Nothing, Countess, nothing."

Gavrilla made a sound under her breath to show she didn't believe her.

"I would like to have more children when Jakub

returns. If not for Daciana still at home, I might go mad."

"Perhaps, my dearest sister," Gavrilla said piously, "We ought to go to Church once we are finished. You've had a great shock and seem not yourself."

Agata couldn't stop the shiver which worked its way up her spine.

Once Bogdan heard word of the attack, he would insist Jakub be told. He might write to him himself. Gleefully spilling Agata's dishonor to all the men under Jakub's command. They would know of her disgrace and Artur had not pressed charges. Agata must write to Jakub herself; she must tell him.

Yet, besides the church, there was no other structure in Râuflor that they could enter without causing excitement for the merchants or scorn of the town leaders. How narrow the path a noblewoman was allowed to walk.

All she said with a bowed head was: "As you wish, Countess."

A traveling minstrel walked out of the bar and through the rows of market booths which filled the square, his bawdy song carried on the wind. How she wished he would shut up. She knew he made his living traveling from town to town. She wondered if he had seen her younger brother and his family. Were they well? But she couldn't bring herself to speak to him.

The first peasants collected their bread with grubby hands and dirty clothing in burlap sacks. The wife told her, "Our family prays for you. It was with sorrow we hear you and Artur Jakubescu were injured, you must be wary of the old Legatus, my lady."

She thanked the family for their kindness. She was blessed for hers. The peasant family went to spend their small wealth on freshly churned butter, vegetables, honey, bundles of herbs and garlic in the rows of booths which filled the square.

Another family came forward. Their heartbeats seemed so loud over the sound of market day. She was so thirsty it seemed to drown her thoughts. The sun seemed too bright. For the first time in her life, Agata hated Râuflor and all its inhabitants.

*

AGATA AND GAVRILLA WALKED TO THE Kirchenburgen, the fortified Catholic Church on the hill. The thick stone walls were large enough to give sanctuary to the entire town, shepherds, hunters, and herdsman, but Agata felt no security.

Daciana skipped in front of the women. Her long black hair swung with her steps in the innocence of girlhood. Too soon, in a decade, perhaps, her hair would be coiled and covered when she became a married woman. Life seemed so transient, naive happiness so fleeting.

The soldiers followed them. Their noisy footsteps pounded on the cobbled stone roads.

Opposite the church was the main entrance to a serene cemetery. She wanted nothing more than to return to her father's county. She had an inexplicable and bizarre impulse to lie on the grave of her mother and sink into the earth, but she was in Jakub's county. The town of which she was born was only five villages to the north, down the main road, but it might be a thousand miles away. Agata had no cart to take her home. She had no horse — and didn't know how to ride even if she did.

The women went inside the church and passed a young novice who swept the stone floor. Incense tickled her nose but did not mask the smell of unwashed serfs sitting in the freshly-waxed wooden pews, speaking to one of the priests. At least the stained glass dimmed the light.

Besides the stations of the cross, every wall was covered in fresco, showing God's love through Jesus. Jesus handed out fish and bread, Jesus with children, Jesus with the bleeding woman, Agata made the sign of the cross and put alms into the poorbox. Gavrilla put her own charity into the box.

"Irina!" Daciana said behind Agata in a voice much too loud for Church.

Agata spun around to quiet her youngest daughter.

"Good day, Countess," Irina curtseyed at Gavrilla first as was custom, but within moments — as the soldiers were outside — the women became a family again. Daciana embraced her sister, who picked her up and kissed her cheek. She curtsied at her mother and kissed her.

They moved into a private prayer room.

"My niece, you're more beautiful by the day," Gavrilla said.

"Thank you, Auntie."

Irina's lush raven hair was groomed in a married woman's coil and covered as Agata and Gavrilla. She smelled the spice of Lexi's trade and Irina's herbal remedies infused into her simply embroidered blouse and skirts. People had always remarked her best feature was her entrancing, eyes the color of twilight: Jakub's eyes. She had his nose too. It was good for a girl to look so much like her father. Agata craved to hold Irina in her arms. Then, she desired her daughter's salty blood.

"Sister, is there more watered wine?" she whispered.

Gavrilla passed her the leather.

She wished to acknowledge her pain to sister-in-law and daughter so they might assure her Jakub's wouldn't direct his wrath at her or at Artur who failed to protect her. He loved them too much. She couldn't bear his adoration or the dishonor she had brought into his house.

"I should think, Irina," Gavrilla said softly. "Your mother needs comfort today."

"Yes, Auntie," Irina said. "Artur sent word to us. Are you all right, Mother?"

"The knowledge my children are safe lightens my heart," Agata said.

"So, she is not all right." Gavrilla put a comforting arm around Agata.

"Right now, the peasants think the Legatus has come," Irina said. "But the sacrifice was not in the field this morning."

"I fear ... " Agata couldn't say the words.

"Perhaps, my sister," Gavrilla said, "Irina should take Cia tonight. You're trying to be strong for your youngest, but there is no need. Let others care for you. Cia, we have a mission for you, a big girl mission."

Daciana answered with the utmost solemnness of a four-year-old. "Yes, my Auntie Countess?"

"Stand at the gate and say hello to anyone who approaches—even if it is a priest."

"Today, you're our strongest and best soldier." Irina handed her a small sheathed knife.

As she had seen Artur do, Daciana pressed her knife to her heart and bowed. Then she took her position.

Agata and Irina knelt at the prayer bench and lit a candle for Jakub together. They prayed for Jakub's return. Irina prayed for her mother's continued health and the return of her wellbeing. Gavrilla prayed for her beloved friend. Agata silently prayed for the ability to regain her honor. Her family's honor. She felt safe in the company of her daughter and sister-by-law.

Unfortunately, the comfortable family moment evaporated when behind them, in a voice much too loud for inside a Church, Daciana said, "Hello, Father Bogdan, my uncle."

The fragrance of a man who had washed in only aromatic smoke for days wafted into the prayer room. Agata thought that was strange. Bogdan regularly washed on Saturday to prepare himself for Sunday Mass. However, she did not smell just Bogdan's scent. She sensed dirty, fetid hay and the musk of animals upon him. *He must have spent the night anointing the sick or delivering last rites to some poor farmer.*

Ignoring Daciana, he bowed. "Countess. How may I be of service?"

"We light candles for my brother-in-law's safe return. We have no need of you at this time." Gavrilla waved him away.

Agata wished Gavrilla would take care around her daughters. Though Gavrilla was protected by the title Countess and Agata was a non-titled Count's daughter which offered some protection, her children were not protected by the nobility. They were commoners.

"Indeed, Countess, you may have no need of me," Father Bogdan said. "But I am sorry to hear of last night's horror, Lady Agata. This is why it is said a woman shouldn't be alone in the night. If you had a husband who was home every night, this wouldn't have happened."

Agata made the sign of the cross before turning to him.

"Thank you. But I wasn't alone. My son, Artur, was with me and our unlucky friend, Robert who cares for my herd. I thank God I have a healthy son to offer me comfort in these trials, my kinswomen and you, Father Bogdan."

The priest cast his eyes upon her and stepped closer. His breath was sour with beer. "Surely if a man can't protect his wife, she has grounds for divorce. A woman of your stature must have other suitors."

Feeling like a doe caught in a hunter's eyes, Agata didn't move. She couldn't speak. Gavrilla moved in front of her. "My sweet sister has no other suitors."

"The serfs say the Legatus has come down from the Mountains to court you," Father Bogdan said. "If he comes for you again tonight, a clear soul will at least allow you to sit at the feet of God. Might I take your confession?"

"Father Bogdan, while we appreciate your concern, if Agata wishes for confession, she will confess to our family priest. We came in to give alms and light candles for our beloved Jakub, not to quarrel with you.

"Leave my sweet sister in peace."

"Count Mihai will hear of your insurrection before God, Countess," Bogdan hissed.

"Please inform my husband you disturbed our prayers for his beloved brother. We might be only women, but there are three of us, we will agree that you interrupted us," Gavrilla said. "As might some young priest wanting to curry favor with the count."

Bogdan lowered his voice. "I still might give you absolution, my cousin's widow." Then he spun around, cassock flying.

Agata felt like all the air had been swept out of the room as Father Bogdan left the prayer room. She clasped herself around the stomach.

"Ignore that fool, Mama. He sought only hateful gossip about Papa," Irina whispered and hugged her about the shoulders.

Agata knew he wanted more. Bogdan wanted what was Jakub's. "I wish to leave this place," she whispered.

"Cia, do you want to sleep at my house tonight?" Irina said.

"Yes!"

"Perhaps Lexi will let Petru off a little early so you might play before the sunset," Irina said.

"You must behave for your sister and brother-in-law," Agata said. "And not be scared, because you'll see me at Mass in the morning, but I won't be able to be with you until midmeal."

"Don't worry, Mama, I'm your bravest solider," Daciana said. "You'll see."

Outside the church, Daciana put the knife in her belt and matched the soldiers' footfalls. As they escorted Irina home, the men quietly chuckled at the diminutive soldier in their midst.

Agata took a few moments to greet her younger son, Petru, her son-in-law, Lexi, and his father, Alexander, but was careful to not take too much of the men's time as the spice shop had many customers.

*

Chapter 4

LYING IN HER BED, AGATA COULD NOT SLEEP. Parched with thirst, her stomach ached by the water she consumed. Loneliness subsisted all around her. She rolled over and felt the cold place where Jakub should be. She squeezed the quilt to her chest. Nausea rose into her throat. *Dear God, let me not be with child. What if my attacker brought the plague to Râuflor? What if he brought a new disease of Venus?*

She wiped her eyes. "And I lost my calf. A calf that might have helped my boys find suitable brides. I can only pray for the heifer to regain her health."

Above, the servants argued. She didn't remember the servants ever speaking so loudly. Did they want her to hear?

"The Legatus came to our town last night," a man said.

"Robert is dead, throat torn open and drained of blood. That's the mark of a strigoi," Another said.

Agata was pretty sure the last voice was Cook.

"I agree. Seven cows are missing. The heifer was badly injured. The calf is dead. Who else could do this except the Legatus?" Another answered.

"But if it was the Legatus, why didn't he take the count's sheep?" The first countered.

She listened across the garden into the bachelor's quarters where Florin interrogated Artur.

"I barely saw our attacker," Artur growled, "But I will duel the first man who slanders my good mother."

The older men assured him that would not be necessary. They all agreed, never was a finer mistress than Lady Agata.

"No matter what happened," Florin said. "Our tongues will not wag."

Their protestations did not assure Agata since tongues were already wagging.

She slipped out of bed and covered herself in a robe. Her feet were cold on the stone floor. She reached for her door, but thinking better of it, she rang for her maid.

Elana's candle flame flickered as she opened her door. "My lady?"

"Come with me to the kitchen? Last night, I had such a fright, I fear going the kitchens on my own, but I didn't eat enough at dinner. The attack and the ugliness with Father Bogdan weighs on my heart."

"Certainly, my lady," Elana said, "If you don't mind me saying so, it is unlucky to quarrel with a priest, the countess ought to be more careful. What if he puts the evil eye on you?"

"I fear thinking of such things," Agata said softly as she embraced herself and rubbed the ache from her arms. Though in reality, she feared Bogdan's loose tongue convincing Mihai that he be permitted to marry Agata and take her house than the evil eye.

Elana put an arm out. Agata allowed herself to be comforted by the other woman closeness. Her stomach cramped in hunger. The scent of Elana's flesh made Agata salivate. Ignoring the urge to bite her maid, Agata crossed the halls of plaster walls. *What if the Legatus is real? What if he attacked me? No. I don't believe in vampires.*

There was power in gold and silver, parsley and garlic, but not because they could ward off vampires.

Infants met death at a midwife's hand because if they were born with a caul, it was thought they were cursed to become vampires. She had witnessed too many instances of infected, untended wounds that might have healed with a good scrubbing of potash soap instead blamed on vampires. Vampires were even blamed when a starving peasant elder failed to recover from a winter's chill when a hot meal might have saved them.

Agata bit the inside of her cheek; trying to pinch the craving away. She looked away from Elana's neck. The pulse within the luscious vein was too much a temptation.

The walls of the long corridor were painted green, but everything seemed black flickering in the candlelight. They passed several tapestries and the carved pillar showing Jakub's family heraldry with his emblem in the cadet position.

They slipped into the kitchen. The maid lit several candles. Light flickered around the room, casting the women in comforting softness.

The two hounds which the manservant kept looked up at them and wagged their tails in unison. The maid sliced off a hunk of yesterday's bread and set in on a plate.

Agata swallowed a bite. It tasted like ash in her mouth. As naturally as she could, she broke the rest of the piece in two and threw it to the dogs. They gobbled up the morsel as if their lives depended on it.

Meat was what her body craved. "Do we have sausage in the pantry?"

"Indeed." Elana sliced pieces of blood sausage and set it on the plate.

The hounds nuzzled her side, hoping for more. She listened to the creatures' heartbeats. Their backs trembled under her hand as she pet them. Her mind wrapped around their primitive dog minds.

Food. Lady. Pet. Food. Food. Lady. Pet. Food.

She threw them pieces of sausage.

"Perhaps some milk or beer would help you sleep?" Elana asked.

Beer sounded awful, but perhaps milk would sooth Agata's stomach. "Would you warm me some milk, please? And for yourself, if you wish it."

*

Chapter 5

AGATA FELT AS IF SHE HADN'T SLEPT AT ALL. SHE couldn't allow the village to know of her weakness, so she rose to her feet. Agata grasped upon the bedframe to stop herself from falling. She couldn't remember ever feeling so dizzy.

She considered her symptoms: exhaustion, unsteadiness, thirst, and strange cravings. She never felt this way when the winter chills ran through the town. She hadn't craved flesh when she was pregnant. She did not have any disease she knew.

What if the peasants are right and there is a Legatus? What if I was attacked by a vampire? Am I one of the damned? Has my hubris set me away from God's path?

Yet, Agata could easily hold her Crucifix as she ever could. Legends said Artemis had cursed the first vampires. Of course, if that were true, why should the Goddess of Wisdom and Craft care about symbols for God the Father, Son, and Holy Ghost?

Another part of the legend claimed vampires couldn't hold silver. Agata touched her most elegant shirt, with real silver and gold embroidery running down the sleeves. Her hand didn't burn.

I'm being stupid.

Outside the window, the trees moved. She felt the wind, not tempered by spring and the smoke in her fireplace whisper to her. The legends said as a vampire, she could become mist. No matter how hard she closed her eyes and dreamed, she did not become mist. She was simply Agata.

Now I'm being unquestionably stupid.

Elana entered her room. "How did you sleep, my lady?"

"Wonderfully after our trip to the kitchen." Agata lied. "Send word to my son. I visit Irina today after Mass."

Agata wasn't even dressed fully when Artur was at her door, his face set in a grimace. She had seen that expression on Count Mihai's countenance several times over the years. It was never good.

"Mother, I must insist you see Father Bogdan and take confession. He informed me about the ugliness in the church yesterday," he said.

"Your dear aunt stopped him from interrupting Irina and I while we prayed for your father," Agata said. "I sup with Irina after Mass. Tell Bogdan he may visit me at the evening meal."

"He says the sun must be up," Artur said.

"Fine. Bring him to me after midmeal then."

"A woman shouldn't dictate to a priest," Artur said.

"Perhaps not, but Bogdan is looking for scandal everywhere so he might find a better position. Your father's position," Agata said. "Do you want him to take this house?"

Artur pinched his lips together. "I know, Mother. He is a fool, but some whisper you lost your honor. Bogdan will use that if he can."

"I did lose my honor," Agata snapped.

He flinched as if she had slapped him. With a voice full of shame, he asked, "What are you going to do?"

"I'm a fallen woman. I must ensure Daciana's future before that is known or find some way to regain my honor. If your father was here ... "

Artur's cheeks flushed. "Lucretia regained her honor by sacrifice and built a Republic."

Agata crossed her arms in front of her chest. "If I follow a heroine from our history, I might follow Chiomara's example, my son."

"That is madness. You're better off with Bogdan." With his uninjured hand, he slapped the door jam and slammed the door hard enough that it shook in its hinges. Once he was gone, she found a cup of spring water and gulped it down.

*

ARTUR ESCORTED AGATA AND THE HOUSEHOLD servants to Mass. Except for his frown, there was no evidence of their argument. She kept her head down as if in prayer as she passed Irina, Lexi, Petru, and Daciana.

Daciana gave her a quick wave, but Irina kept her younger sister close.

In the second to front row, Agata genuflected. She easily looked at the Crucifix. She held her prayer book and hymnal, but all she could reflect upon was her unending thirst.

Trying to think of anything else, she thought about her argument with Artur. *Does my son expect me to commit suicide as Lucretia did?*

Since that wasn't going to happen, she pondered the legend of Chiomara. She might discover the man who attacked her. She might kill her rapist and regain her honor as the legendary queen did. Agata imagined herself climbing the Carpathians. *How could I go into the mountains? How could I take any man's head? I've never picked up a sword.*

Since her marriage, she had never left Râuflor. Before she had only been in her father's county. If she braved the mountains, whether the Legatus was an enterprise brigand, dishonored merchant, or vampire: how would she take his head?

Bogdan's eyes remained on the second row where she sat with her son. With a practiced face, he hid his emotions, but his body emanated rage. Artur was right. He didn't like being dictated to by women. Even the slightest analysis of the man showed Bogdan would make a terrible husband. However, in the depths of her mind, she wondered how he would taste if she bit him hard enough to make him bleed. *He probably tastes like sacrilege with a hint of slothful idleness.*

*

ACCOMPANIED BY ELANA AND FLORIN, AGATA took a basket of Cook's rose petal honey cakes to Irina's. The sunlight seemed even more violent today than the day before. In the market square, the two thieves still sat in the stocks. She wanted to offer them comfort but couldn't chance it when her own reputation had been blemished. Merchant Street was nearly empty as it often was on the Sabbath. Behind the row of shops, she could hear people inside the wooden houses and garden plots. Riotous noises carried through the alley and created a clamor with a mass of its own.

She turned the corner and spied Irina and Daciana playing with a ball in front of Irina's house. Looking at her two daughters, warmth spread across her heart, and she felt as if she had smiled for the first time since the attack.

"Mama!" Daciana ran towards Agata.

Agata lifted her daughter up and kissed her. "Were you a good girl?"

"Yes," Daciana said. "Lexi and Petru played Little Rabbits with me, and Lexi let me ride on his back."

"He looks forward to the day he is a father," Irina said. "He will be a good father, I think."

"Yes, a tender spirit and generosity to children are the finest attributes of a man." Agata waved at Lexi, Lexi's father and Petru in the garden as they collected herbs for some potion or spice blend.

It is good, Agata thought, I*rina has a husband who is home.*

As she had previously, she sensed the steady rhythm of her own sweet daughters' heartbeats. Below Irina's a softer third heartbeat.

"Are you with child?"

"We don't know. Perhaps. I haven't bled this month," Irina whispered and made the Sign of the Cross to protect herself and the unborn child from any passing devils. The women and servants went inside her house.

Since Irina only kept a single charwoman, she poured watered wine. Agata opened her basket of rose petal cakes and a round of soft cheese.

After helping set the table, Daciana sat on Agata's lap, chattering nearly non-stop about the day's adventures until the men came inside. Agata wondered what Irina had told her husband and father-in-law.

"Mother of my new daughter," Alexander inclined his head to her took his chair, and lit his pipe.

"Father of my new son," Agata replied and inclined her head.

Petru's curly brown hair fell into his face as he bowed to his mother. His father's eyes stared at her in sadness. She ignored the smell of his skin; his hair. He stiffened as she embraced him, but that was the way of apprentice-aged men.

"I need you to keep Daciana longer. Artur insists Father Bogdan visit me tonight." Though it was a family lunch, she was careful to use Bogdan's title in front of Alexander and Lexi. The town's head priest and cousin of a count was a man to respect and fear.

"Don't worry, Mama," Irina said.

She couldn't think of a better way to tell her children, so she said it openly: "While I don't remember the entire attack, I drank a parsley potion."

Petru's face reddened, and he clenched his fists.

Alexander spoke: "The whole town knows the Legatus came down from the Mountains, Lady Agata. It doesn't change our goodwill towards you. Whether it was he or another man: we would kill the fiend if we could."

Agata lifted her head and met his eyes, hoping she appeared confident to her children and in-laws. "I will recover my honor before Jakub returns. I ask you to keep my little girl safe. Even from me, if I fail, and I become something I am not."

"Mama, you never believed in vampires," Irina said.

"I may have been wrong," Agata said. "I do still believe people blame vampires when they should look to ill air, but that doesn't mean the Legatus doesn't exist as well. Or someone pretending to be the Legatus. I mean to discover who is in the mountain and take his head, if I can."

Irina wrapped her arm around Agata. "Mama, don't speak of such things."

"My lady, you don't have to prove your honor," Lexi said. "Vampires only leave their tombs at night. You walk in the day. You're not a vampire."

"I still must prove my honor. Swear to me that Daciana will be safe from all devils."

"We'll keep Cia safe," Petru said. His tone sounded more like a man's by the day.

"Irina's sister is my sister by law and by my heart," Lexi said.

"Your family is tied to mine," Alexander said. "Jakub Petrescu Christian is a great knight. He will never fail you or your children by setting you aside."

While she appreciated the kind words, Agata asked, "If I don't return, you will keep my daughters safe?"

Lexi glanced at Irina. He held his silver medallion to her. "I swear it, Lady Agata. We will find her a good husband when she is of age. And if whatever fate befell you, if it happened to Irina, I would not turn my back on her. I love her too much.

Lexi's speech did not alter her mind any more than Alexander's words had.

She embraced Petru. "I'm proud of the man you're becoming. Your aunt and brother will have your father's instructions on your future bride."

She embraced and kissed her daughters in turn. She hugged Lexi.

"Be well, all of you."

Escorted by her servants, Agata walked away from the house.

Daciana cried for her. Agata's heart ached for her youngest, but she kept walking. She might not know what happened to her or even if she genuinely was a vampire, but when she embraced her children and smelled their sweet flesh, the thirst grew more intense.

*

Chapter 6

WITH ARTUR AND THE SERVANTS WATCHING, Bogdan held his Crucifix as if it was a shield against Agata. "Back, wife of Jakub, if that's who you are." He thrust open the curtains and chalked the sign of the cross on the floorboards. "Or are you the wife of the devil?"

Agata stood in the fading sunlight. She tried not to squint, but the afternoon sun was so warm. She and Artur knelt in front of the priest. Though Agata trembled, she reminded herself silently, *I'm the wife of Jakub, not the wife of the devil. My children's mother. A midwife and dairywoman. Being a vampire doesn't change that.*

She smelled the rank of Bogdan's sweat as his greasy hand placed a wooden cross on Artur's brow. It made no sense, he usually bathed on Saturday nights to prepare himself for Mass.

"Confess Artur Jakubescu."

"When we were attacked, I was disarmed and failed my mother and our herdsman. Though my mother taught me well, I have a fuller sense, a man's sense, of duty before God." Artur trembled with tears in his eyes, which did not fall. "I think the man thought he killed me before he attacked my mother."

Bogdan smiled, exposing his stained teeth.

Agata refused to quiver as he placed a wooden cross on her brow. He asked for her confession.

"I have nothing to confess, but I fear my body tempted

an attacker. I fear I was dishonored, but I don't know. I want to tell my beloved husband first, but he is away at war."

Bogdan leered at her. "The Lord God will not allow an honorable woman to be dishonored."

That was a blatantly false statement. There was coughing from the doorway.

"There are several instances in the Bible where honorable women are raped through no fault of their own," Cook said.

Artur's eyes pinched closed for a moment. Then he cleared his throat. "Indeed, Princess Tamara ... "

The priest narrowed his eyes at Artur and cut the words from the air with a wave of his hand. "You both lived. You both say you blacked out. This means you're not a witness, Artur. You do not know what happened. Perhaps your mother bargained to the devils who attacked you to let you live. She gave the only thing that was hers to give."

Artur gasped. "Mother, is that true?"

Her body felt hot. Artur was young and might cling to anything to forgo shame. "No. I did not give myself to anyone."

Bogdan's lips creased into a deep sneer. "The question remains: are you an honorable woman or not? Think of your sons before you answer."

"I don't remember the attack. I fear ... I fear." Agata trembled. "But I don't know. I don't remember anything."

Cook lifted her hand towards Agata and then lowered it.

"Why do you hide the truth?" Father Bogdan smiled a wicked and terrible smile and looked around. "Artur is grown. He has an appointment with the count. You will have no protection."

"My husband will return to me," she said.

"Your husband is dead. Marry me and allow me to

lead this household, I will protect you in peace. If you don't, then I suppose I could bring charges of adultery upon you to the town council."

"My mother is innocent!" Artur exclaimed.

"Innocence doesn't matter," Agata said softly. "He is not threatening me with a lashing, or even death. He is threatening us with scandal." She met Bogdan's face and considered his words. "I do not know my husband is dead. I have no heard word for seven months from him or anyone. If he had fallen in battle, his company priest would write to me. If I am to remarry, I must have confirmation my husband is dead."

"What if it was the Legatus who attacked her?" Artur said in a small voice. "She would be innocent!"

"All of you leave this room," Bogdan said.

Agata stood very still for a moment. She knew this might happen; she should have prepared for it. She should have hidden Florin behind a tapestry.

Bogdan stared at her when clenched teeth. "This could have been avoided if you had just remarried. I would have left my marriage to the Church to protect our family. Then, woman, you would have had a protector."

"I will stand for the wife of Jakub," Florin hissed. "She has been a fair and kind mistress."

"And I will cut you down," Father Bogdan said, tapping the knife on his belt. "Does a servant believe he can stand before God's representative?"

Agata stood and moved between them. "Florin, do not let yourself be harmed. This house is just wood and stone, but you're a friend and excellent servant. Go with my son and help him in his studies."

Florin seethed but said through his teeth. "As it pleases, my lady."

"Son, take the servants into your uncle's home, take my surviving livestock, the count has a copy of Jakub's direction on your and your brother's future," Agata whispered. "Lexi and Irina will keep Cia close, but you must protect her."

Artur nodded. He dropped his eyes. His face was full of sorrow. "I will, Mother."

Agata raised her head and looked at her servants. "The good and kind Father means to bring charges of adultery on behalf of my beloved husband, Jakub. My only witness was my beloved son, who was also assaulted, so his witness is not to be trusted."

"What will you do, my lady?" Florin asked.

"I mean to regain my honor if I can, or I will find death if I cannot. I ask you to forgive me for leaving you all who I am so fond."

She could not show pain, only bravery. She grabbed her son tightly and embraced them. "I remember the day of your birth. I love you, and I am proud. Go to your honorable uncle, and live well, my son.

"Find situations for all who rely upon us."

"Enough!" Bogdan shouted. "It has been many years since the Legatus has harmed a soul in the county, due to our Good Count's sacrifice. However, there is one way to know if it was him." Bogdan pulled a small box from his robes. Inside were Hosts.

"The body of Christ will destroy your demons."

"Amen," Agata said.

He turned to the others. "Leave all of you."

Agata's heart sunk into her stomach as she watched them scurry out in fear of the priest. Maybe she should have let Florin fight him.

Bodgan tied Agata's hands together as if she was praying. He walked around her spilling scented oil and holy water upon her shoulders.

"The Body of Christ."

Agata opened her mouth and expected him to lay

a Host on her dry tongue. Instead, he stacked several between his fingers and pressed them into her mouth. He smashed his meaty hand over her face, squeezing her mouth shut.

Choking, she tried to pull away. Her mouth tasted full of ash, just as it had with the regular bread.

Agata stared at the priest in loathing. *It is he, God's own messenger who has desecrated the Host. If he had believed her unclean than how could he handle Jesus's flesh in such a way*

Agata forced herself to let her saliva wet the Hosts and gently work their way down her throat. She wanted to gag as the dry alter bread scratched her esophagus, but she must not desecrate the Host. She lowered her eyes to the floor and swallowed another piece. Then another.

"Now, you'll listen."

He put his hand to her breast. She yanked her body away, her mouth filled with half-wetted Hosts. She tried to swallow.

Bogdan kicked her squarely in the back. She choked on the paste and crumbs.

"If you won't give me this house, I'll just take it." He leaned close: "All I wanted was an industrious wife. A wife of Proverbs. Your husband is dead. Yet you still struggle. Take me as your husband, and I'll let you live."

She shook her head and tried to kick him. Her tongue coated with Host paste; she just wanted to breathe.

He whispered: "You still defy me? I would've been a good husband. I would've let your children live. Now I will take Jakub's house and his wife's reputation just as I took the sheep from the sacrificial fields."

"Why?" She gasped, spitting crumbs onto her beautiful carpets.

"Because Jakub is nothing more than a fancy-dressed bully. Shining armor and a warhorse doesn't change the boy. He left this parish with everything; he will come home to nothing. That's what God promised me when I saw the sheep in the field."

"Jakub's alive ... "

Bogdan's hands wrapped around her throat. He squeezed. Her hands tied together, Agata could not find any leverage. She scratched his hands, and she pushed ineffectually on his grip.

He squeezed tighter. "If Jakub is alive, I would have preferred for him to come home and see his wife in my bed, but having a dead wife who was defiled is just as well."

Please, God, whatever happens to me, protect my children.

Her windpipe was crushed by meaty hands. She stopped struggling as God lifted her spirit from her earthly form. For a moment, the world went dim. She felt as if she was singing a donia; the lyrics were happy. If Jakub were dead, she would be reunited with him in heaven.

Bogdan dropped her corpse onto the floor. "Fool woman. All you had to do is marry me." He kicked her.

Agata knew her body was dead, but she felt the foot hit her stomach. She could still hear, still see, even think. She knew it was imperative she did not move, not yet. *Let him think he won.*

Bogdan opened her chamber door to the crowded hallway.

"Artur was right. His mother was attacked by the Legatus; she became a vampire. The Flesh of our Lord destroyed her." Bogdan gestured to the body.

Listening to her son and the women of the household cry, Agata thought her heart would shatter, but she could not weep. She must not react at all.

His voice rising in triumph, Bogdan said, "I will return with a coffin, stake, and brick to ensure eternal rest. I will exorcise this house of any further demons. Florin, bar the doors. I suggest the rest of you leave as Lady Agata suggested earlier."

*

Chapter 7

AGATA FEARED WAITING. SHE DIDN'T KNOW when Bogdan would return. Still, she listened to the pounding of boards on the front door and chains drop the portcullis. It would be over soon. The servants were gone. Artur had gone to his uncles. The other children were safe. That's all that mattered.

She tried to look at her injured neck, but no longer had a reflection in her mirror.

She found her silver and gold blouse and brushed her fingers against it. Surprised by the heat, she pressed her reddened fingers into a salve.

"Hmmm. Why didn't it burn me yesterday?" She spoke aloud the most logical answer. "Yesterday I wasn't dead."

She dressed in three layers, placing the blouse with real silver embroidery in the middle, she covered her hair with her plain maramă and packed her best. She put her gold Crucifix around her neck. It didn't bother her in the slightest. She packed her medicine bag.

Out of habit, Agata carefully locked the windows to the manor. Perhaps it didn't matter. The poor or more likely Bogdan would raze the house soon enough, perhaps even the servants would make off with whatever treasures they found, but it felt good to lock the windows. Normal. She was the Mistress of the manor, and she would protect it as Proverbs said she should.

In the kitchen, Agata ate her fill of sausage and stuffed the rest in a bag. She found a bucket with a piece of touchwood and straw. She lit the straw, and when the fungus caught the shouldering ember, she loosely fit the lid so as not to kill the low flame. Listening to the men on the street-facing side of the house, she left through her garden door. Expecting an attack, she stayed near the wall and then sprinted to the apple tree. She ducked low to remain behind her garden and plucked several herbs that were supposed to protect people from the walking dead.

She crossed her old herdland. Her surviving cows grazed lazily at the spring flowers which pushed through the grass. She never had felt as lonely as she had this moment.

If she was indeed a vampire, she had no people, no family anymore. Bogdan had seen to that. She was sure she had died an unnatural death. Death by priest probably made it more aberrant, but was the method of her death how she became a vampire?

There were many ways to become a vampire in the legends, but none seemed to fit her circumstances. She had been baptized. She wasn't born with a caul, an extra nipple, a tail, or excess hair and was doomed to become a vampire as the myths claimed. She wasn't the seventh child. Her mother ate salt during pregnancy.

Shaking these thoughts from her head, Agata silently prayed to the Blessed Virgin to protect her children, and she would regain her honor. She slipped noiselessly into the weir to remain out of sight of the shepherds tending their flocks. It was dangerous to move about the woods at night. If vampires were real than no doubt, other things roamed the forest. Perhaps the Ottoman's God and Djinn were also real. Maybe the Fair and Earth Spirits were real. If vampires were real, there must be truth in all legends.

Agata followed the meadow-covered foothills to the

ancient Roman footpath, which led into the mountains. She carefully found her footing on the narrow trail twisting over the rocky hills. Sharp angular rocks stabbed her feet through her leather shoes. She wished she didn't feel the chill. What was the point of being undead if she felt cold?

She smelled death on the air. As she moved across the path, she found torn pieces of a cow. Only scraps of flesh remained on the bones so she couldn't identify if it was one of hers.

She pushed a branch out of her face and moved on.

The forest was not silent as one might think it would be. Noise filled the wood, just beyond Agata's sight. The gentle step of animals, nightbirds took wing and hunted.

The night grew late, and Agata's brain swam in a sleepy fog.

The rocky ground became covered in patchy snow. Snowdrop blossoms pushed out under the patches of snow. She thought of her children hanging Mărţişors in the apple tree. There were no Mărţişors in the mountains.

Dawn lightened the sky. Her eyes grew blurry and teared; light blinded her. She felt faint. She was so thirsty.

She needed blood and a safe place to sleep. *I must hide from the sun, but first I must eat.*

She gathered a few sticks and lit a small fire from her smoldering torchwood. She melted some snow.

The water did nothing to quench her thirst. Agata ate the rest of her sausage. She groaned with a pang of voracious hunger.

Nearby, Agata observed a rabbit, nibbling on a dew-covered blade of grass. As if the spirit of a wolf had taken her soul, she dashed towards it, moving faster and faster. Before it could escape, she dove upon it and raised it to her lips. Her gums screamed as she felt her teeth expand for the first time.

The poor creature scratched her face as it struggled.

Blood flowed into her mouth and echoed in her veins. Her humors sang in joyous rapture. She felt stronger than she had since the attack.

Once it weakened, she broke its neck and bit into its sweet flesh.

She found shelter in the hollow of an old tree. She picked up a heavy pine bough and covered the opening. She dreamed of her beloved Jakub and their children. She did not know if he was alive or dead, but she could never see her family again. The rabbit proved she was damned. She hoped her children would forgive her for leaving, but no doubt they would be told to forget her. She was dead.

The sun crept higher in the sky.

She pushed herself deeper into the hollow, covered her face with her veil, closed her eyes, and tried to sleep.

She felt a strong instinct to bury herself in the soft loamy earth, but she did not want to dirty her clothes any more than the journey already had.

The wind pushed the clouds and branches. Panic caused her heart to flutter and legs to twitch as the sun move over her hiding place. She clenched her eyes shut and reminded herself she was safer in the tree than she had been in her own house with Father Bogdan shoving Hosts down her parched throat.

Agata drifted off, thirsting for more blood than a rabbit's body could hold. She awoke what felt like minutes later by a sunbeam moving across her cheek. She yelped as she felt the warmth. She tucked her face deeper into her woolens and tried to move the branches to provide better protection. The sun passed. Had she imagined that?

With a spark of inspiration, she slipped her left hand from her glove. She put it into the sun. Her skin itched, then smoked. She pulled her hand back and rubbed a cooling unguent upon her hand.

The sun had reddened her skin before, and she had

many farmers whose skin had peeled after a long day in the fields. She had never been scorched. So the myth about the sun was true.

Speaking aloud eased her fear. "Our people have so many vampire myths. Perhaps, I shall find a less fatal remedy than Bogdan's? Or perhaps I will make remedies for vampires."

She chuckled at the thought.

*

Chapter 8

THE SUN FINALLY LOWERED BEHIND THE mountain. With luck, she could make it to the old Roman fort before the sun rose again. If the Legatus of the Mountains was a vampire, soon she would know it. If he was just a human using the myth, she would know it. She pushed away the pine boughs and clambered from the hollow. Her outer skirt was filthy and covered in blood, her blouse was bloody, but her inner clothes were unsoiled.

Agata climbed higher. Icy wind gusted and blew sticks and pine needles across her path, stinging her exposed skin. She crossed a slope of snow-capped boulders where the pines grew twisted and more desolate. The night air sparkled. The tips of the tree branches were lined with ice and frozen moss. The patches of snow became fields of snow. She picked up a large stick and pushed it into the snow. Agata traversed the barren earth with care as the snow hid that the ground was pockmarked with holes, some small enough to catch an ankle, others large enough she might fall into and disappear.

Through the trees, Agata caught sight of the gloomy four towers of the old Roman lookout. She wanted to run towards the apparition. She wanted to know if the stone was solid or a phantasm? She kept her pace, refusing to arrive any more tired, injured, or dirty than she already was.

She did not know what she would find.

The north side of the fort was piled with snow, and the eastern wall had crumbled down the hillside. Needleless, skeletal branches twisted away from the fort. As she moved closer, she picked her way through broken siege engines, dented shields, swords, and pikes stained with ancient blood and rust. She observed Latin words carved into broken stone and found several carved phallic symbols as the Roman soldiers were known to keep as talismans.

She gazed at the darkened arched windows scattered across the walls and wondered if the occupants could see her approach. If so, she hoped they looked at her from the windows rather than the arrow slits. Squeezing between rotting wet wood and mossy stone, she passed through a broken portcullis. The ground of the keep was slippery with mud, gravel, and the ghostly feet of a thousand men which had broken down the earth and left it unsuitable for crops.

The inner keep was protected by an ornately carved door emblazoned by a knocker in the shape of a lion. She knocked and waited. No one answered.

She knocked again and looked to the east. The sun would rise shortly, then it would crest the wall. She must hide from the sun. She pushed on the door. Unlocked! She went inside and closed it behind her.

"Good day?"

No one answered.

Inside the fort was as cold as it was outside. Agata's soft footsteps squeaked under the old cracked stone tiles.

She found a tarnished brass candelabra sitting on a dusty table covered in multi colors of ancient wax. She lit the remaining candles and used the flickering warmth to her hands.

More Latin words were inscribed on the threshold.

The wall across from the front door was covered by

a large mural of presumably the Legatus. He stood over a battlefield, his enemies, his enemies' dogs and horses, and city lay waste.

"Who are you?" A raspy voice said. She jumped as a man with a bent back in a dirty, blacken tunic came from the shadows. Around his neck was his only sign of wealth: an amulet of silver. His hair was still thick but graying. His skin looked sallow. His hands were gnarled, his nails were yellowed. Yet he seemed too young to know the ravages of age. She felt his heartbeat in the air.

She was sure he was human.

She introduced herself. "Agata Arturescu Vidraru, wife of Jakub Petruescu, a Knight of Christendom. I've come to meet the man who stole my honor."

"The other vampires are there, up the stairs, Honorable Lady. They rarely come down except when it suits them," the servant said, in a strange accent.

"Thank you." *So there are more vampires than just the Legatus.* That may or may not be to her advantage. "How many vampires are there?"

"You will be the sixth," the man whispered. "Be wary."

"And what is your name, friend?"

"Titus Octavia Zelina, Honorable Lady."

She noted he used his mother and grandmother's names as his surname, rather than a father's. And he said it in the old Roman way rather than the contemporary manner.

"Thank you, Titus Octavia Zelina."

*

Chapter 9

AGATA CLIMBED THE STEPS AND MOVED through a heavy, wooden door with carved panels which looked gray due to a blanket of dust. She felt the warmth as she entered what once must have been a lavish great hall. Three fireplaces were lit and cast dim light around the room. The plaster was cracked and falling off the stone. Old Roman shields painted with mythical beasts lined the walls. The glass in the leaded frames was cracked and broken and covered in rotting wool blankets.

Yet, life was everywhere. Spiders lived in every corner. Rats scurried along the walls. Pigeons and sparrows fluttered in the rafters.

Death aboded in the fort as well. Five vampires turned towards her. One man — *could it truly be the Legatus of the Mountains?* — sat in a marble chair surrounded by two carved stone wolves. Three women sat on cushions near his feet. They had different skin tones, but their complexions suggested death, or something unnatural.

Nearby on a wooden stool sat her rapist. Somehow, she instinctively knew her attacker the moment she laid eyes on him. Almost at once, as she had known her own mother, she felt connected to the man on a strange level. This attachment filled her with self-loathing. *Focus. This might be one of the vampire's tricks,* she thought. She remembered his rancid breath on her body during the attack and redirected her fury back to him.

His threadbare clothing rotted off his frame, and he looked like he had not taken a bath in over a decade. The edging on his shirt was yellowed. His red coat was frayed. He was tall and thin, handsome in an understated way. His skin was ashen, stark against his brassy blond hair. The blue in his veins seemed to complement his brilliant blue eyes. She knew his name without asking: Nicheloa Augustus Flavius, another Roman.

The Legatus's booming laughter rang to the rafters and started the living creatures in the hall.

She didn't see Nicheloa move but smelled his putrid breath whispered beside her face. "So you have come to us?"

"You took my honor; I have come to claim it."

"We've no honor here — at least in the limited way you define it. On your knees before the Legatus of Carpathia, woman," Nicheloa hissed. "The Legatus claimed he felt the creation of another vampire."

"How dare you, I am Agata, wife ... "

"You're the least of us; take your place at your master's feet." With his hand on the back of her neck, he dragged her across the hall towards a throne. With his greater strength and weight, he forced her to her belly.

"This woman comes to you, my Legatus."

Agata elbowed Nicheloa until he released her. She scrambled to her feet and rose her chin to meet the vampire's gaze. "I am Agata, Daughter of Count Artur Vidraru, the wife of Jakub Petrescu Christian. Who do I have the honor of addressing?"

The Legatus of the Mountains appeared to be a man in his prime, but there was something ancient in his face. A twisted lump spoiled his otherwise aquiline nose. His tanned complexion had an undertone of blue, a symptom of death. His piercing brown eyes were nearly hidden under bushy eyebrows and his unbrushed thick mane of black curls, short beard and mustache over took his stern and terrifying face. He was not tall for a man, but his broad shoulders and muscular arms were exposed by his Roman style tunics rotting off his body. His undertunic was torn thin gray linen —perhaps it was once white— its frayed hem was dirty and blackened. His brown outer tunic looked like it once might have been red. It seemed too cold for such thin garments.

"I am Gaius Lepidus Severus, Legatus of the Carpathian Mountains. Do you throw yourself upon my mercy as did my other concubines?"

He gestured at the three vampire women, but his piercing eyes didn't leave her face.

The women's uncanny expressions showed nothing but disapproval and sadness. They watched, not speaking. Two were darker skinned, luminous brown eyes and long free black hair that hung freely down their backs. They appeared to be most likely in their twenties. The other was pale with blond hair and blue eyes. She seemed to be the same age as Irina and bore bruises around her neck from someone's cruelty. With three beauties, she doubted Gaius would be interested in a thirty-two-year-old mother of five.

"I need no mercy. I am a lady of honor. I have no master save the Lord Above and my husband whom I promised to love, honor, obey with a kind heart on the day of our marriage," Agata said.

"You're brave but foolish. Crawl to me," Gaius said.

She refused to even lower her gaze. "Even my husband would not dare order me to crawl, or he would find his next meal poisoned."

Gaius stroked his chin. "You're no noble here. Just a lesser vampire, made by a lesser vampire. If you want my protection, show me your hair."

Agata didn't comply; Nicheloa ripped off her maramă. The linen fell to the stone floor. She refused to cry as he unraveled her coils and plaits.

"Another raven beauty and not a touch a gray," Gaius said. "Though you're rather old, you're still pretty enough. You may be my fourth concubine."

"I've entered in no such arrangement with you; I stand before you as the wife of Jakub," Agata said.

"You bore me, woman. Kneel."

Agata felt her knees buckle, she locked them in place. *Gaius and Nicheloa are spoiled children,* she told herself. *I will not kneel.* His mind slithered over hers. It felt as if a thousand insects crawled up her feet, legs, back and over her hair. She would not be cowed.

Seconds later, she was on her knees.

The women didn't move or even blink.

From her prostrate position, Agata said. "My people call you the Legatus of the Mountains. Is that a self-appointed rank?"

Gaius rose to his feet.

"Are you the warrior in the mural below or are you simply a leader of frightened women?"

His fangs expanded as his face twisted with rage. His mind slipped away from hers. The sensation of insects on her flesh disappeared. Domination was forgotten for the time being. He raised his hand as if he would strike her. "Was it your husband who wrung your neck? Look upon my women, and you can see I am not above such things."

She hid her trembling hands under her long sleeve. *Gaius exists in the ignorant darkness which brought forth the collapse of the old Empire.*

Gaius walked around her, studying her. "I didn't create you, but I will keep you. If you exist in pain, it is because people make their own misfortunes."

"If you truly are a Legatus, is Nicheloa your Lictor?" Agata asked.

"Yes."

"Then, I challenge you for my honor and freedom."

The women's eyes moved quickly. They glanced at each other, then to Gaius, Nicheloa, Agata, back to Gaius.

"With swords, axes? Have you ever held a weapon in your delicate hands? I might crush you."

"With the weapon of my choice, when I win, you will do what I ask of you," Agata said.

"A woman's weapon is always poison," Gaius said. "And nothing can poison me."

"I'm a learned midwife."

"Even a midwife cannot poison a vampire," Nicheloa said.

"I bring forth life while you live in a tomb with the rats and spiders," Agata said. "You have no idea what I know."

"So be it. When I win, I'll torture you until I bore of it," Gauis said.

With those words, his women drew closer to one another. The pale one covered her throat. They feared Gaius. Nicheloa's eyes dropped. He also feared him though his experience as a soldier made him better at hiding it.

"It might be centuries until I bore of you." Gaius smiled.

Agata has seen terrible wickedness before in men. Gaius thought she was a plaything and assumed she would lose. To him: the challenge was a diversion to break up the centuries. These fiends are beyond worthless.

"As for weapons, I choose the quality of my own mind," Agata said.

"A woman's mind, what good is that?"

Though she wanted to school him, she did not speak of ancient texts or legends. "When I win, I want my freedom and honor returned to me."

Gaius waved his hand in a listless gesture. "Yes, yes. So this battle of wits commences. What shall we do, tell riddles?"

"No. I will heal your servant and remake this dungeon into a home in a week."

Gaius's eyes opened wide. "How is this a battle of wits? What woman's trickery is this?"

Agata did not answer him. "My first question: What is the remedy for your servant, Titus Octavia Zelina's, ailment?"

"Why would I care? He's just a servant." Gaius said. "He's a human; humans die."

"Is that your answer?" Agata hid her elation at his confusion.

"I suppose you have such knowledge," he said with scorn.

Below him, one of the women with raven hair pulled the younger pale woman close to her breast. The other shifted between them and Gaius as if they expected him to harm the girl.

"As I warned you, I'm a midwife," Agata said calmly.

"Perhaps, you should have insisted upon the riddles, my legatus." Nicheloa smiled with his blue eyes. He, too, found Agata's challenging diverting, but he was a different type of man than the Legatus. "Besides, even if you lose this woman's challenge, don't forget you won our bet that I created a vampire."

Agata felt a connection with Nicheloa again. She ignored it.

Gaius calmed and chuckled. "You are correct, my friend."

Nicheloa said, "I'm poorer since you lived. I have no way to keep a woman without my lord's blessing."

Agata considered it was wrong to overlook Nicheloa, especially since she was planning to kill him. To him, she said, "I was made poorer since you stole my cows." Then to Gaius, "Titus Octavia Zelina has the sailor's disease."

"Prove it," Nicheloa said.

"Goodman, pray to tell me do your joints ache?"

Titus looked at Gaius in terror.

"Answer the woman's questions," Gaius said.

"Joint pain, Lady," Titus said.

"And pray, how old are you?" Agata asked.

"One and thirty."

"Open your mouth. I'm wagering my freedom your tongue is spotted," Agata said.

Titus's gums were bleeding, and several teeth had been lost. His tongue was covered in spots.

Gauis's sneer disappeared.

"I must make him and all your human servants a needle broth. Though it is sharp in taste, they must drink it for one week, but we will see an improvement within days," Agata said. "Titus, please collect stems of new-growth pine. New growth is a lighter, brighter green."

"My Legatus?" Titus asked.

"Do as the woman asks. I want to observe the miracle of a human who grows strong again," Gauis said.

*

Chapter 10

OTHER THAN THE BIT OF SHOUTING OF A WOMAN'S trickery, which sprinkled dust from the rafters onto the stone floor, Agata was happy. There had been no violence. The sun rose higher in the sky. Eventually, the Legatus and Lictor went down the stairs to the old barracks.

"Gaius doesn't come into the harem. You will be safe there. Come," the woman with long straight black hair said. "He calls it a place for the weak. Still, take care with your words, Titus is not our ally and his daughter, Ulpia, is dawdling and slow."

Agata wasn't sure if she could trust the concubines or servants, but she had no other choice. "I am called Agata."

"So we heard. I am Sylvia, that is Phillipa, and the golden one is Julia."

Her long black hair spilling freely, Sylvia opened the carved door. The harem's stone walls reflected filtered light. Mold hid in the corners and between the stones. Carpet beetles scurried before Agata's steps.

Phillipa closed the first set of shutters, casting the room in greater darkness. Over the screens, the sheer linen moved across its rail. Velvet curtains drifted slower. It didn't take long for the room to fill with stale, musty air.

The women ignored the furniture and lay on the floor. Agata could see why. The rotting leather didn't look like it would hold their weight anymore. She didn't want to place her face on the musty rug or a moldy cushion but saw no other choice. She reclined on the floor with the other women. On the east wall sat a shrine covered in figures of the old pagan Goddesses from the Empire. Pots filled with cosmetics, ribbons, combs and womanly apparel sat on shelves. Discarded ripped fabrics and crockery lay in the corners.

This close, even in the darkness, she could see the bruises on the pale girl's neck were deep and purple. Agata's heart went out to her. She touched her own neck. "May I help you, Julia? I have a salve."

The younger woman didn't meet her eyes.

"Your remedies will only help so much. What she needs is blood," Phillipa said. "We have been forbidden to give it to her. Gaius keeps Julia in penance."

"Still, I might help the pain. I have my own bruises."

Agata opened her case and rubbed a salve upon her neck.

"You were strangled too?" Phillipa said. "Not by Nicheloa, that's not how he takes women."

"Was Gaius, correct? Was it your husband?" Sylvia asked.

"No. My husband is at war. I was alive after Nicheloa raped me, but our parish priest killed me, claiming I was a vampire."

Phillipa chuckled. "And he was right. You are a vampire."

"It was an excuse," Agata said softly. "The priest actually just wanted my house."

"Men always want something," Sylvia said.

Julia glanced over at Phillipa.

"If you think it will help even with the pain, Julia wants to try the salve," Phillipa said.

Agata gestured for Julia to sit in front of her. "The home I built with my husband is in the western shadow of the highest peak, where are you all from?"

"My mother is Breton-born, she came with her lady as a maid, I was born somewhere close." Julia lifted her pale hair off her shoulders so Agata could dab the unguent on the back of her neck where Gaius's fingertips had drilled into her flesh.

"I am from Spain," Sylvia said. "I was stolen from my people and taken to the Capital. And Phillipa is from Rome. She is the eldest of us. Nearly as old as Gaius."

"You're his wife?" Agata asked.

"A freedwoman. He changed me for his pleasure." The disgust in her voice was apparent. "Then he claimed me as his concubine."

Finishing her ministrations, Agata wondered if she should tell the women there was no more Empire. Did they know of the spread of Christianity throughout Europe or the centuries of invasions the Goths, Mongols, and Ottomans?

Sylvia said, "I don't think any man or woman has rejected him since. He doesn't like it. It's better to just accept Gaius; he isn't a terrible lover."

"I'm the wife of Jakub." Agata moved a cushion and yelped as a rat raced towards the wall.

"Now you're the concubine of Gaius," Phillipa said softly. "Fight as you will, but Gauis will have you.

"Gaius does not follow the Roman order of things. He does not care if your Jakub has had you or Nicheloa or that you bore children. All that matters is now you're a vampire of his bloodline. He claimed you as his. It brings him a twisted joy to take something from Nicheloa."

"But if I win the challenge?" Agata whispered.

Phillipa sighed and picked up a comb to plait Julia's golden hair.

Sylvia shook her head. "He won't let you win."

"But I must win," Agata said. Searching through the discarded and broken items in the corner, she found a pot which used to hold some sweet-smelling cosmetic. Not knowing what used to be in, she set it aside; she needed clean crockery if her remedy was to work.

"Don't worry about his threats of torture," Sylvia said. "Torture doesn't interest him. He will have you a few times and grow bored. However, he won't let you go. He feeds us, clothes us in silk when Nicheloa can find it, protects us from the changing world.

"All he asks in return is to make love on occasion and Phillipa to dance for him. When she is well, Julia will sing. I will play my flute. Perhaps, there is something you can do to entertain him. Otherwise, he leaves us to our pleasures."

Agata was careful to not show her thoughts, but she wondered what pleasure was found in a rotting old fort.

Sylvia apparently didn't like her silence. "Let us muse for a moment. If Gaius lets you win, what prize will you ask for? Will you ask to be his wife so you might rule over us?"

"No. I will ask to go home with proof of my honor."

Phillipa's mind wrapped around Agata's. It was soft and cold as if fresh snow was falling upon her cheeks, yet it was terrifying to have one's own spirit eclipsed by another stronger will. Thankfully it was over quickly.

"She tells the truth," Phillipa said to the other women. "She thinks if she finds her honor, her husband's family won't forsake her."

"How sad." Sylvia shook her head.

Phillipa looked over Julia's shoulder. "Agata, you must realize if your husband doesn't forsake you, he must forsake your children. Let him go. Stay here and be the Legatus's concubine. One man is rather like another after a few centuries."

"I thought a Legatus leads men?" Agata asked. "On horses."

"He used to have men with horses, but they died long ago. Now there is only Nicheloa," Phillipa said.

"Well, there's one other thing," Julia whispered.

"Hush, Julia," Phillipa tapped the top of her head with the comb. "Speak no word that might be used to harm you." She finished the braid and tied it into a bun. Then wrapped it in a long cloth.

"Is that why you're being punished? Did you try to kill Gaius?" Agata asked.

Julia shook her head. "I'm not brave enough. I ran away."

Phillipa drew the younger woman closer to her. "But she won't again."

There was a knock on the door. A skinny young girl probably no older than nine popped her head in. Her tangled hair hung about her shoulders. Her Roman style toga praetexta was threadbare as was the faded purple band around her waist. Around her neck was a silver amulet to ward off malevolence.

"Lady, my father asked me to bring you this basket." She bowed and left.

Agata looked inside and found pine needles of good quality. "Where do I get water?"

Sylvia gently touched Agata's wrist and drew her close. "We will not help you destroy our coven. Besides, the old well is dry."

"We've no need for water," Phillipa said. "We drink blood."

Agata adjusted her layers of clothing. She would have liked to strangle the vampire women for their acceptance of their fate, but she needed allies.

"I don't want to destroy your coven. All I want is my honor. You've human servants—even if we don't need water—they do," Agata said. "There must be a source."

Julia motioned to a rope hanging from the ceiling in the corner.

Silently cursing herself for her stupidity, Agata rang

the servants' bell. The young girl reentered, trembling, and holding her elbows close to her body.

"I need water, girl," Agata said in a tone that meant she was to be obeyed. "Finish the task and report back directly."

"Yes, Lady." The girl scurried in haste as if a devil was behind her.

"Agata, the girl, and her father are slow in the mind," Phillipa said languidly. "Don't be cross with them. Come sleep. The sun is out, but there's always a new moonrise."

Agata declined.

The other women made themselves comfortable and warm in the shadows.

Once Agata was sure the other women slept, she removed her lower layers of clothing and hid them in a broken wardrobe. If the other women wanted her things, she might lose all that was hers, but they seemed uninterested.

The concubines must want something. Julia ran away for some reason. Sylvia and Phillipa were compelling in the way, intelligent women always were. They knew something or wanted something more than this quiet harem filled with rats and bugs, but what?

Ulpia returned, carrying two full buckets in her small strong hands. "Do you need more, Lady?"

"I need a clean pot. I'm trying to make a tonic to heal your father."

The girl followed her directions to the letter.

Ulpia was not slow as the concubines warned her. She poured the bucket of water into the pot and set the pot to boil.

Agata removed the brown papery sheaths from the base of the needle. Not wanting to let the other women know of her knife, she tore the needles into smaller pieces and crushed them between her hands. She put the needles in the pot of boiling water and let them steep for five minutes.

Agata took a sip to ensure the potency. “Now, Ulpia, bring me to your father, so I might help him.”

*

Chapter 11

HOLDING THE STILL-HOT POT OF PINE-NEEDLE tonic, Agata followed the scrawny girl down the long dirty corridors to the fort's old scullery. A tallow lamp hung from the ceiling, casting light around the room.

She passed large jars marked lanoline or oil lining the wall. Blocks of ice and snow melted in large troughs which were drained into old barrels.

She noted how Titus or some other servant had stacked a smaller brick to create a small firepit inside the large ancient fireplace. Sheepskin pallets lay inside the structure. From the ceiling hung silver amulets and old clothing.

Agata wiped a dusty pewter cup and poured Titus a dose of tonic. Titus grimaced as he sniffed it.

"Drink for your daughter, if not for yourself. And the child must drink as well. It will stop any of your bad air harming her lungs."

"But I don't want it," Ulpia whined.

Titus threw his head back and drank the tea. He handed Agata back the cup. She poured another dose for the girl.

"Drink, Ulpia; the lady commands it," Titus said.

"But, Papa, we put pine on the dead."

He patted her shoulder. "Drink."

"It smells gross."

"No. It's not the best-tasting thing," Titus admitted,

"But it will make you strong, ocella."

"But ... "

Titus's voice changed as he scolded, "Ulpia Titus Octavia, if I have to tell you again, you ... ,"

Ulpia didn't wait to hear her father's threat. She tilted her head back and gulped it as fast as she could. "Yuck!" she cried.

"You can drink milk or water as you wish now," Agata said. "Are there any other servants in the fort?"

"Not any longer." Titus poured the girl a cup of water. She drank it just as fast.

"Any longer?" Agata asked.

"Ulpia, ask the lady what your next job is," Titus said with a look at the girl's head. He would not speak in front of her. Her life might be hard; he wouldn't make her harder.

"What should I do next, Lady?" Ulpia asked.

"Have you any vinegar?" Agata asked.

"No," Titus said.

"Gather more needles. This time the color doesn't matter. We will boil them and wash the walls and floors with the solution. I also need a bucket of ash and fat from a slaughtered animal. We will be making soap. It's fun."

Ulpia scurried to do her bidding.

"Tell me of the others," Agata ordered.

"The Lictor finds infants left out by farmers." Titus went on to explain how in a lean famine year; the vampires ate the infants.

"How cruel."

"They are killed quickly, and with mercy, more mercy than their fathers gave them when they're set out to freeze," Titus said. "However, at times, the Legatus decides not to kill them. He brings me a child to serve the vampires. How or why he makes the decision, I do not know."

"So she is not yours?"

"I've never known a woman. You don't have to

fear me, Honorable One. I'm a eunuch. All the boys are eunuchs. Other than the Lictor, the Legatus, doesn't keep intact men around his women."

"You've had other children?"

"They died just as the other children died when I was a child. There's little food and vampires can be cruel. I keep a strict watch over Ulpia. She's past the most vulnerable age. She has gone hungry too many times to ever become a true beauty which should protect her from the Lictor's vileness when she is older."

"And the Legatus?" Agata asked.

Titus sighed. "The Legatus keeps women out of habit. He will keep you safe; he will make love to you on occasion. He will feed you and the other women the blood of the cows and sheep which he receives in tribute. Do as he says and you've nothing to fear from him."

"What do you eat?" Agata asked.

He explained how some meat is thrown towards the servants, but he set snares for rats and rabbits. Ulpia collected berries and mushrooms when she could find them, but very little grew on the mountains.

"I will write this recipe for a tea down for you and your generations of children. It will keep them strong when they can't find berries," Agata said.

"Thank you, Honorable One," Titus said.

*

THE SUN WAS HIGH. UNABLE TO SLEEP AND wanting to know more about this strange place, Agata followed Ulpia, who held a wreath of pine down a long dark hallway. The skinny girl knelt before an open hole with generations of human and animal bones. She invoked

Artemis and several other childhood Gods and dropped the wreath upon the bones. "I feared I would have to throw Papa in there. I'm glad you're making him better, Lady."

"You heard me behind you?" Agata said.

Ulpia turned. "Vampires become more silent with age, yet I must know where their feet fall. Papa taught me."

"You're a clever, industrious girl, but you don't fear us?"

"Why would fear one of you wretched things?" Ulpia said. "I'm Ulpia, daughter of Titus, son of Octavia, daughter of Zelina, daughter of Crassus, onward for millennia. All I must do is keep to the light."

"I see the wisdom in your words."

"The sun is up. If you don't sleep, eventually, you will go mad and run into the sun like the other vampires. The harem is safe from the Lictor. The Legatus never visits it; when he wants you, he calls you to his room in the barracks." She spoke in a jaded, wearied voice which sounded too old for a young girl's lips.

"I still have work to do," Agata said.

"Even a vampire needs sleep to work," Ulpia said. "I'll take you back to the harem until nightfall."

Agata lay beside Julia, who lay beside Phillipa. Half-asleep, Julia cuddled towards her and wrapped her arms around her and rested her cheek on Agata's shoulder.

Staring at the darkened ceiling, Agata tried closing her eyes. It did not matter. Eventually, she rolled to her side and pulled Julia closer. She wept for the wounded young woman she barely knew, her own children, her destroyed cattle and everything else she had lost. Eventually, an uneasy sleep took her.

Agata's dreamed of millions of insects, spiders, and rats biting her, crawling inside her and eating her innards: deget by deget, palmă by palmă. The vermin took over her body.

She awoke with Phillipa shaking her shoulder. Her perfect ringed curls draped over her, like snakes. Agata shuddered and pushed the image from her mind.

Agata sat up. Beside her, Julia still slept. Phillipa gestured for her to follow. "Walk with me. The sun is setting."

Phillipa led her to a shuttered balcony. Agata held back for a moment, but the other woman walked out first. "You need not fear. The sun is down."

The sky was streaked with lavender. Below the mountain, the valley was dark, but single points of warm light broke up the darkness. Agata wished she knew which town was hers, but she didn't. From this position, she didn't even know if she was facing west or east.

"I witnessed your plot when I looked into your mind. You mourn your lost life and put yourself on a fool's errand," Phillipa said.

Agata tried to turn away, but Phillipa gripped her wrist with a surprising amount of strength.

"You will stop me?"

"Only if you harm my sisters," Phillipa released her. "I speak to you as another mother. Julia fills the place which has been empty since my daughters' deaths. I protected her from Gaius's anger when she ran away. She has not been forgiven. I will kill you if you endanger her place in the coven."

"I have no intention..."

"I don't care about your intentions. Your passions play a dangerous game. More dangerous than you realize. There have been other concubines and soldiers. When they betrayed him, Gaius tossed them into the sun or worse."

Agata opened her mouth. "I ... " she stopped and asked an intelligent question: "How many others were there?"

"In a thousand years? I've lost count. At least,

hundreds. Gaius had them burnt to ash."

"Then, what is your counsel?"

"Forget your errand," Phillipa said. "Heal Titus if it pleases you to do so, but forget your task."

"You had children?" Agata asked her. "You must understand I want to go home."

"You can't," Phillipa said. "If you love your husband and children: you must not go home. Never. Even if you regain your honor, you still cannot have the life you had."

"Jakub will not forsake me if I have my honor. His family ... " Agata took a deep breath.

Phillipa squeezed her arm gently. "You will harm them. Your need for blood will grow. You are fighting it now. To come into eternity with you, Jakub will have to also leave your children. Let him remarry, grow old. Let him die with the children as my husband died."

"But I cannot fail. Gaius will torture me if he wins."

"He won't if you throw yourself on his mercy," Phillipa said. "You're surprising naive in the mind for a mother over thirty."

Since she didn't have a handkerchief, Agata wiped her nose with her hand. She sensed there was more to Phillipa's counsel, but she did not have her gifts. She wished she did.

Phillipa sighed. "No, you don't. It's confusing to hear others' emotions, thoughts, and spoken words. People often feel about several ways about any given subject. Their thoughts pound upon my mind.

"It's quiet here in this fort. A learned woman such as yourself must see the value in that for someone like me. Perhaps I don't love Gaius anymore; perhaps I do. Sylvia is right, there are worse men in the world."

*

Chapter 12

AGATA'S EARS RANG WITH PHILLIPA'S COUNSEL. She didn't know what to do, so she set to cleaning the harem. Lounging amongst the cushions, Phillipa, Sylvia, and Julia watched Agata and Ulpia chase rats from the harem with a broom.

"Why are you doing this?" Julia asked.

"Are any of them pets?" Agata asked.

"No."

"Then I'm getting them out of here."

"Gaius probably won't even see this room," Phillipa said. "Gaius likes things the way they are."

"She tries to curry our favor," Sylvia said. "Daughter of a Count indeed. Perhaps you're the servant of a Count."

Panting from the excursion, Agata stopped. "I am who I claimed to be. That fiend isn't the only reason I'm doing this. I don't want to live in rat feces, spiders, and fleas."

"No disease can harm vampires. The fleas don't even bite us. They want warmer blood," Phillipa said.

"But Titus and Ulpia might be harmed by illness." Seeing their uncaring expressions, she added quickly, "Please tell me you do not enjoy sleeping with the rats and spiders."

"Of course not, but eventually you'll also tire of human work."

Phillipa stood. Sylvia followed her out of the harem

arm in arm. “Julia?”

“I think I’ll help Agata,” Julia said softly.

“Remember what I told you,” Phillipa warned. Agata wasn’t sure if that was directed at her or Julia.

The younger woman nodded and picked up a pile of old broken crockery from the corner and set it in the basket which Agata was putting ripped and broken things. After she finished, she took the spiders from their webs and set them outside the window.

Her gentle hands surprised Agata, yet twice the hands made the work lighter.

“How did you come here?”

Julia glanced out the door first. No one was there. Then out the window. “I was laundress, and Gaius saw my golden hair and became enamored. He had Nicheloa steal me from my home.”

“Do you want to go home?” Agata asked.

“My mother is dead,” Julia said. “Titus’s mother Octavia was younger than Ulpia when Nicheloa brought me here.”

“Then why did you run away?”

She pinched her lips together. “Boredom, I guess. I thought I’d have a better life, but a week on the mountain, eating rabbits, being cold and afraid of the sun, of the villages, even running into Nicheloa and his demon horse, I returned.

“Gaius was angry at me. He yelled so loud I feared the fort might come down on our heads. I accepted being chastised — Phillipa didn’t let him really injure me — and we all go on with our existence.”

“Are you happy?”

“I exist,” Julia said. “I’m not sure vampires can be happy, but I love my sisters.”

Agata separated the torn linen from the rest to re-stuff the harem cushions.

"Do you remember how he turned you?"

Julia looked out the door again.

"Nicheloa raped me," Agata said. "But I don't comprehend how I was turned. I've thought about it many times as I climbed the mountain. My people have many myths about the vampire.

"Some claim vampires are born with a caul, must be the seventh child of the same sex in a family and lead a life of sin, die without being married, die by execution for perjury or suicide or from a witch's curse."

Julia's laugh was musical. "I wasn't married, but I don't even know any witches. Do you?"

"No."

"Gaius took my blood from my wrist, then he told me not to be afraid and bit me over my heart. He held me close as I bled into him. My heart stopped. He then gave me more of his blood. I was dead, but not. Then he gave me the blood of a boy because I was so ravenous that I ached."

So the myth about biting over the heart is true, Agata thought.

"How strange. That isn't what happened to me at all. Except I knew I was dead, but not and very thirsty."

"I don't know much about it. Gaius made it clear I was not allowed to transform anyone. He says I'm too young. He is less restrictive with Phillipa ... but ... "

"He's the head of this House," Agata finished.

"And expects to be obeyed," Julia nodded. "Phillipa can trick him into doing what she wants most of the time."

"She seems very wise."

"She is," Julia said. "And she's always been kind to me."

Titus entered the harem. "Honorable Ladies, the Legatus of Carpathia orders you to the hall."

Agata hated leaving work half-done, but she knew it was essential to conform and observe. As they entered,

Phillipa and Sylvia sat quietly on their cushions. Phillipa had a slight look of triumph on her face. Agata hoped she had not made a fatal mistake by speaking to the youngest and least educated vampire.

"Julia, come here," Gaius ordered.

Julia glanced at Phillipa but hurried to him. She gasped as he pulled her onto his lap. He combed Julia's long blonde hair with his fingers.

"I was told you are helping Agata with her task," Gaius said.

She sat perfectly still. "Yes."

"Why?"

Her eyes were wide and panicked. "It's something to do. Different, Legatus."

His finger traced her pink ear, but his eyes were on Agata. "You oppose with my methods, Agata."

"I don't know your methods."

"It causes you distress to see marks on Julia's neck. Phillipa said you tried a salve on her last day."

"Cato the Elder said, 'the man who struck his wife or child, laid violent hands on the holiest of holy things. Also that he thought it more praiseworthy to be a good husband than a good senator.' "

"Cato the Elder did not have to teach a rebellious vampire," Gaius said. "What would you have done? Let this vampire roam, hungry? Eventually, she would have attacked a village, perhaps the one with your beloved husband and children in it."

Agata didn't answer him.

"Phillipa and Sylvia cause no problems because they experienced life before they were transformed. Nicheloa and I are the same. Even you, in your state of rebellion, are working to make our world more inhabitable, not less. But Julia was made from a woman who was still half a girl.

"You have had children. Did you not teach them to

obey?"

"Yes, but there are better ways than with bruises," Agata said.

"If the marks displease you so, I will remove them." He opened his wrist and told Julia to drink. She pressed her lips to his wrist. She swallowed his blood and cried out. As if it was magic, the bruises around her neck vanished. The flesh of her neck became immaculate.

"You see, I'm not an ogre."

"Thank you."

Gaius stood up and told Julia to return to her sisters, which she did. "What else can I do for you? Should I remove the bruises from your neck? Is this why you couldn't bear to see the young one chastised because your husband did the same to you?"

"My husband is a great knight on the front lines of battle. He does not know my fate." Agata said. A single bloody tear rolled down her cheek. She wiped it away.

He stepped closer to Agata.

"Don't touch me."

Gaius's voice was soft. "Your love for your husband is heart-wrenching to watch, but he will forsake you. He must. If he remained with you, your hunger would eventually kill him."

Her voice trembled as sorrow overtook her entire body. "Let me return to my work. I will be washing the linens and cushions in the harem so they might dry in the day's sun."

"I won't see the harem."

Agata put her hands on her hips. "You may be the ruler of this house, but you're not the only one who lives here. As long as I live here, I won't sleep with rats."

There was a moment in which the concubines stopped breathing.

Gaius laughed. "I dismiss you to return to your efforts.

Julia, remain with your sisters."

Phillipa left her cushion and wrapped her arms around his. "Gaius, you always say a person makes their own misery. If Julia's punishment is over, please, may she have a little freedom? Agata is her sister too, and will no doubt keep an eye on her.

"Let Julia know the old pleasure of a job well done. You know how her young heart craves more affection than we can provide.

"Did you know Agata has a daughter no older than Julia was? The girl is newly married and pregnant with a grandchild."

"Is it any wonder Agata acts so irrationally?" Sylvia took his other arm. "And you never blame a newly-formed vampire for senselessness human passions."

"Ah, very well. Whatever gratifies my concubines satisfies me," he said.

In her mind, Phillipa's voice rang out as if she had spoken. *However, be clear, Agata, you're not above Julia. Julia works as she wishes.*

Dismissed, Agata left the hall. Julia silently followed.

Agata was pleased the young vampire's wounds were healed but felt used. In truth, she was even more confused about Phillipa and Sylvia's intentions.

*

Chapter 13

GOING ROOM BY ROOM, AGATA, TITUS, AND ULPIA washed the ceilings, walls, and floors with pine-needle solvent. The bricks bled with rust. Most of the rooms were abandoned and neglected. The tiles were littered with leaves and old bones of victims. Bugs and dust flew off the ancient carpets as they were beaten. The leather and wooden furniture were rubbed with lanoline until they gleamed. Anything so damaged it wouldn't hold her weight was dissembled for parts or burned as fuel.

Old threadbare cushions, rags, and tattered fabrics were soaked in water and pine oil and left on the roof to dry, collected again after nightfall. Once dry, Agata started to re-stuff and wrapped cushions, but Sylvia surprised her.

"I know how to sew. I will help with this task, but only this task," she said.

Julia assisted as she liked. Agata noticed when Nicheloa was around the fort, she stayed near Phillipa. When he was out collecting the sacrifices, she happily chased bugs and rats. Her most effective action was to collect all the broken crockery and till the soil next to the old kitchen. She lined the patch of tilled earth with the broken pottery to make a garden for Titus, Ulpia, and any future human children.

As Agata moved through the fort, she found an old trove of weapons and dead husks of men, long mummified in banded iron armor stacked on their rectangular shields.

Their swords and pikes at their sides covered in a thousand years of rust, dust, and spiderwebs.

"Thinking of using those?" Nicheloa asked behind her.

Ulpia dropped her rag and scurried behind Agata. "Leave me be; you are frightening my helper." Agata did not stop scrubbing rat droppings off the floor.

"I will not harm you; you're my legatus's woman."

"If I am a woman of Gaius, you have already harmed me." She dreamed of reaching for a pike and decapitating Nicheloa where he stood. Between her lack of instruction and his training, Nicheloa would crush her within seconds. *Keep your own head.* "Who are these men?"

"Former legionnaires," he said.

She looked up from her cleaning. "Why are they here? Were they vampires too?"

"A woman knows nothing of esprit de corps. They gave themselves to Gaius after he was turned." His voice was devoid of the emotion of brotherhood of which he spoke.

"So, though you carry the title of lictor, you're an errand boy. You deliver the sacrifice, steal him women when he wants."

"A man needs a job, and Gaius hasn't needed a bodyguard for centuries."

Agata stood up and stretched her back. She wished she did not feel connected to Nicheloa. "Ulpia, go help your father."

Ulpia gladly escaped the room.

Nicheloa was taller than she, but she looked him in the face. "Why did you make me a vampire?"

He looked away. "I didn't mean to create you."

She moved, so she was in front of him again. "Tell me."

Nicheloa's ran his fingers through his short beard

and grimaced. "It will pain you to relive it. Forget it happened and go on with your existence or walk into the sun. If it pleases you, know Gaius upbraided me for my carelessness."

"Tell me."

"The sacrifice wasn't in its field, so I went to find another. A vampire can't be soft on such things. I saw your cows. Then your man ran out of the small barn like a rabbit.

"Robert wasn't my man. He was my herdsman."

"Regardless, the stank of his fear was delicious. Do you know how much blood and flesh are in a grown man? I was so excited to have it all for myself, and Fideles, my horse. I felt as if I were an Emperor myself!

"Then your boy shouted. If I hadn't drunk from the herdsman first, neither of you would have lived. I left your herdsman for Fideles." His eye grew dreamy. He touched the scabbarded dagger on his belt, his fingers lingered on the leather. "Besting the boy was nothing. However, I prefer a soft woman over boys. I dominated him so he would sleep until morning and took you."

"Since I killed the herdsman, I assumed you were a widow. Who cares about the rape and murder of a herdsman's widow? So, yes, I took you, but let your son live, relatively unscathed. You should be happy." She wondered why he was defending his actions. He obviously believed raping her wasn't a crime — especially after destroying the man he assumed was her husband.

Agata said, "The herdsman died, but the boy lived. Will they become vampires?"

"I didn't spill my blood or seed on them, so no," Nicheloa said. "I obviously spilled something in you. You ought to thank me."

"I thank you for my son's life." Her voice cracked.

His tone grew soft. "You're my creation. I caused you pain once; I won't do it again."

"Don't mock me. You took me from my family and now claim I belong to another man." Fighting her urge to weep, she threw her rag at Nicheloa. He stepped out of the way before it hit him and landed on the floor with a splat.

"I do not mock you." Nicheloa picked up her rag and returned it to her. "I only mean I didn't want to change you. I dominated your mind. You were supposed to die. You weren't supposed to wake as a living vampire, to be killed by a priest, and walk in death for eternity."

"My husband, Jakub, is a Calvary officer; protecting our land from the Ottomans. I am not a widow. You raped a married woman," she accused him. "You claim to know esprit de corps. That means you should call Jakub your brother too. You raped your brother's wife." Agata's sniffed, fighting tears.

"Yet, your Jakub isn't here, is he? He left you alone." He stepped closer. "How long had it been since your husband found peace in your arms? A year? Longer?

"I took you, so don't bother lying. How long had it been since he even looked upon you?" He pressed the line which had taken residence above her eyebrow. "Has he seen that?"

Agata pushed away the lump in her throat.

"You're a vampire now. Among vampires, you simply are Agata. You will live forever as young as you are today. Why you wish to be a charwoman is beyond me.

"If you want Jakub, seek him out. You already know he will forsake you. Isn't that why you came here? The count's daughter; the soldier's wife, you know you would be cast aside. You are adrift."

She pushed him away from her. "I came to claim my honor as Chiomara did!"

Nicheloa laughed. "And you believe you will have my head by scrubbing floors?"

Agata went back to her work. "I don't have a plan, yet.

But I will not allow Gaius to have me."

"You should," Nicheloa said. "Join your sisters in the harem. Gaius will lavish you in gold and fine fabrics when I can find them. The beasts he collects are for you and the other women. He eats the heart; I eat the kidneys. The rest is yours, the horses, and servants."

"However, if you belittle his generosity, if you continually disobey Gaius, as others did before you, he will have me kill you in some terrible way. Our horses will feast on your flesh and blood so as not to waste such a treasure."

"Phillipa told me there were other concubines."

"Yes. There have been mistakes in a thousand years which we lived. I am not a fool, Agata, or I would be dead. You may spin remedies rather than turn a song, but that means you are useful to this coven. Your presence might mean our servants live into old age. However, this work is beneath you."

"Perhaps, this work is beneath me, but if I don't do it, who will? There aren't enough servants to keep the fort."

"Then I'll find you servants." He bowed and turned away. At the door, he said, "I am sorry for the pain I caused you."

"I don't care if you're sorry!" The tears came then, too powerful to stop. Blood spilled upon her cheeks, her blouse, her freshly washed floor.

From the hallway, she heard Titus speak: "Lictor, the Legatus of Carpathia orders dinner."

From the door, he bowed. "Honorable One, you've been summoned to the hall. Please don't cry. Everything is well." He wiped away her tears with a clean rag.

Agata followed Titus to the Great Hall. Gaius sat in his throne. His eyes did not alight upon her any more than he watched Phillipa dance. Agata did not doubt he ordered it. Her veils spun around her. Her long brown legs kicked upward and then she jumped, so high she seemed to soar.

Julia and Sylvia watched her with appreciation, at least.

There was a fourth cushion set beside the other women. Agata sat on it. Wooden goblets stood on a tray beside the throne.

Nicheloa brought in the warhorses first. Their fanged mouths clattered in anticipation. Their eerie neighs and snorts echoed over the stone.

"Nocte and Fideles," Slyvia whispered to Agata.

Nocte was black with white socks and a white blaze. Fideles was a gray. Used to carrying armored men, both horses bodies were heavily muscled. Their manes glimmered in the candlelight.

"May I, Gaius?" Julia asked.

He waved at her in a bored manner. "As it pleases you."

Julia crept to the horses with her hands out towards them. The animals were obviously used to the girl, but Agata felt uneasy as their fangs nipped at her fingers.

Nicheola brought in one of Agata's cows.

Did no one care that I love the creature? That I brought her into the world so my sons and daughters might inherit wealth since they are provided nothing else as a birthright. She did not bother speaking the question aloud since she knew the answer.

Gaius clapped. "Enough dancing. Now, my women, the Lictor has brought us a cow. Enjoy my generosity."

Julia went back to her cushion as did Phillipa.

Nicheloa set two long wooden troughs in front of the tethered cow. He pulled a knife from his belt. He slit the cow's throat. She took a step and fell, bleeding into a trough. Agata could not stop her pounding heart as she watched the scarlet drain into the gutters. One for the human vampires and one for the horse vampires. Her mouth watered, but she did not move, she was so mesmerized by the blood.

Sylvia groaned in hunger beside her. She glanced

at her companions. The women's eyes grew wide, but Gaius's face did not change. There was no emotion behind generosity. He didn't even take pleasure in it. Just as Titus and the women informed her, Gaius did perfunctory services to his underling, because it was expected of him and kept the peace.

Nicheloa sliced into the cow's belly; her entrails fell onto the floor.

The concubines left their cushions and jumped upon it and tore its dead flesh.

"Will you not eat, Agata?" Gaius whispered. "You must be hungry with your exertions." His will overcame her resistance.

Agata found herself kneeling beside the other women and eating pieces of fresh intestine, sucking the blood from the muscle.

They took their cups and dipped it into their trough. The drinking of blood brought laughter. She drank the scarlet liquid and found it more pleasurable than the most exceptional wine. With every gulp, injuries she had suffered disappeared. Her body knitted itself back together.

However, Agata refused to lose her mind to the bloodlust. She watched how, blade in hand, Nicheloa cut out the cow's heart. He carried the bloody heart to Gaius.

His pupils dilated and his fangs expanded. He took a bite. Blood streamed down his face, and for the first time, Agata saw exquisite joy in his eyes.

His task done, Nicheloa knelt beside Agata. He bit into the cow's kidneys. All this was done without words or instruction. All ingrained habits.

*

AFTER DEVOURING THE HEART, GAIUS ROSE

from his throne.

Agata followed him. “Thank you for insisting I drink from the river of living waters.”

His eyes studied her. “Those are strange words.”

So Gaius did not know scripture, interesting. “Do you not know the story of Jesus?” Agata asked.

“I was already a vampire and striking bargains with your ancestors when the prophet of Judea and his cult spread throughout Rome. Your faith is a strange one, but I do not tell my concubines who to worship. A Christian woman ought to be obedient as a Roman woman.”

Agata said cautiously, “I wanted the blood, but didn’t. I felt your encouragement. I don’t know why, but after I drank, it felt as if the bruises on my neck are gone.”

He brushed her hair off her shoulders. He did not balk at her crucifix anymore than she had. “They have yellowed and are healing. That was just a cow, but the more blood you drink, the quicker you’ll heal. My blood is the living waters as you put it. I can heal you if you’ll be mine.”

“But I love Jakub.”

“More’s the pity. But you will forget him in time,” Gaius said. “However, remember I won’t wait forever for your broken heart to heal. You will be mine when I call you.”

Agata figured saying nothing was better than arguing. He placed his hands upon her shoulders. When she didn’t respond to his touch, Gaius pushed her away and returned to his quarters without requesting any of the women’s company.

Agata returned to her errands and kept mental notes.

The vampires and servants could consumed most of the cow’s organs in one day. The rest of the blood was drained for tomorrow, and the muscles were hung for several weeks later.

As requested, Titus carved the fat for making soap

and candles. The skin was soaked and hung outside to tan.

*

Chapter 14

THE SUN HAD RISEN WHEN AGATA HAD RETURNED to the harem. Though she was satiated by the cow's blood, her hands and back ached. Julia lay sleeping, her head on Phillipa's lap who held her and stroked her hair. Sylvia met Phillipa's eyes. She rose and slinked across the carpeted floor. She wrapped her arms around Agata and pulled her to the floor. Agata did not fight as Sylvia covered them both in a rug.

"It was idiotic to reject Gaius."

"I love Jakub and I want my family back."

"Then kill the Lictor and return to humanity. Return to your children if you can," she whispered. "Gaius might not know what village you are from, but remember, Nicheloa does."

"I can't kill him."

"Your heart is going soft?"

"No. I'm not physically strong enough, but I still plan to have my vengeance. I must use my mind," Agata whispered.

"Good." Sylvia smiled. "If you mean what you say ..." she paused. "I could live in eternity without men to tell us what to do. I would be Phillipa's lictor."

It sounded like the truth. Agata wondered if it were a trap or a hint they would help her. She wanted to believe the women thought of her as one of their own. By her conversations, she already understood vampires did not have human principles.

Sylvia pressed her lips against Agata's. "If Phillipa ruled, we would live justly. You might stay here safe with us." Her soft black hair fell upon her flesh and tickled her.

Agata whispered, "I've only kissed Jakub like that. Gaius ... "

"Doesn't share us with men, but what we do with each other in the walls of the harem is not his concern. No vampire remains innocent. Not even that one." Her eyes flickered over Agata's shoulder to where Phillipa sat with Julia. "Gaius bores of them quickly when they are created that young. They never last long. If Phillipa didn't love her so, Julia would have met her final death decades ago."

"I feel your desire," Agata whispered. "But I can't fulfill it; my heart belongs to another."

"Then rest well." Sylvia slipped out of the rug.

Agata watched as Sylvia returned Phillipa. As kind as any mother, Phillipa lifted Julia off of her lap and tucked her under a rug. She kissed the girl's brow.

"You could still join us?" Phillipa said.

"No, thank you."

Arm in arm, the older women went to the other side of the harem for their pleasure and no doubt whispers.

Once the harem was quiet except snores and rhythmic breathing, Agata counted to one hundred. Still no noise. She rose. She crept across the room and checked the wardrobe. Her clothing and medicine kit were not touched. She removed her silver embroidered blouse. Wearing gloves, she carefully ripped the first seam holding the left sleeve onto the bodice. She loosened the threads on the second seam. It should rip easily.

*

Chapter 15

MOST OF THE BOOKS IN THE OLD LIBRARY WERE nothing but torn vellum and rotten leather. Many wax tablets were cracked with age. However, Agata found a wooden box filled with letters on parchment. She peeked through them. She could read Latin quickly enough, even if some of the sentence structure of the old Empire were strange to her.

The letters told the story of the newly transformed Gaius requesting military help from his father, a senator.

Gaius admitted he had hired the wrong prostitute. At first, he believed he was cursed by Venus in the medical way, but the blood lust grew until he killed his private physician and later his steward. He drank from captives, but when they ran out, his soldiers sacrificed themselves to feed him.

In the next letter, Gaius explained how he turned his officers and "a modest Roman woman whom the Gods gifted unnatural intuition."

Another letter informed Gaius his father was dead. By the dates, Gaius still wrote to his father's ghost. Over the centuries, he turned women for his men, and he experimented on the vampires who didn't obey his will.

Agata paused. There was noise in the hallway. She left the letters and went back to scrubbing the wall.

"What are you doing in here?" Gaius roared. As he entered, he pushed Ulpia out of his way, knocking her into the wall.

Titus glared at his master. There was palatable hate in his eyes, but the eunuch said nothing.

Agata dropped her rag into the bucket. She hurriedly crossed the room and picked the whimpering girl up. She checked the bump on her head and then kissed her forehead. "You're all right."

The girl cringed, so Agata gently passed her to her father. He wrapped his arms around his daughter and drew her close to his chest.

She stared at Gaius and hoped her rage forced insects to crawl in his brain. "Though many of these books are already dust and droppings, I shall stop the rats from eating these volumes. If you do not wish us to clean this space, we will leave."

"It's fine. I generally don't find women near the barracks when I don't call them."

"It's not fine," Agata said. "You are not to speak to me in such a way, nor should you knock down little children. You might have killed her."

Gaius growled: "Then we would drink her blood. She's nothing to me, and you're losing importance by the night."

Titus's face grew purple with rage, but Gaius didn't turn towards the man.

"I am not afraid of you, Gaius," she hissed.

He grabbed her shoulder. "You should be."

Expecting a slap, she ducked away from him and covered her face. He pushed her away from him.

"Clean this room as you will. Run your errands as if you were still a human woman, I do not care, but do not disturb me again."

Once he stormed away, Agata asked. "Are you all right, sweet girl?"

Ulpia nodded.

To Titus, she said, "Do you want to take her to her pallet?"

"No, Honorable One, she seems to be fine."

Ulpia and Titus returned to their chore.

Agata returned to the letters which became a journal of sorts. She must learn what it was to be a vampire. She discovered Gaius once had a male concubine who ran away. He cut off the lad's hands and feet. Though he did not cauterize the wounds, the man did not bleed out, but crawled around until Gaius reattached his feet and hands. Interesting.

Agata wondered what else she might cut off and a vampire would still live. Perhaps Gaius would let her have Nicheloa's head if she didn't kill him.

⁕

Chapter 16

THE REST OF THE WEEK FLEW BY. THE VAMPIRES feasted on the cow's remnants each twilight. Each night, Agata wondered if she had bitten off more of a job than humanly possible. When doubt pressed against her heart, she looked to Titus, who had grown strong again.

The old fort became livable: even for the undead.

As she faced her seventh dawn in the harem, Agata carefully dressed in her delicate silver threaded blouse.

She stood in front of Gaius. "In seven nights, I created a habitable home for you and healed your servant, Legatus, now I expect you to keep your bargain."

"You want to be my wife?" he asked. "Is that why you are dressed so fine?"

"Hardly. I am the wife of Jakub," she said, not hiding her disgust.

"What does the younger son of a count rate to a legatus? Your own count sends me vassalage each full moon as did your father."

"But I love my husband; I don't love you," Agata said.

"I do not require your love. I require your obedience," Gaius said. "You must learn that if you are to survive eternity. Just as you must learn though you love him, your husband will forsake you as required by your strange faith."

"Which is why I will take Nicheloa's head to show my husband that my honor was bestowed. I don't want to harm another soul, but I must have my honor following the example of Chiomara."

"What?" Gaius's fangs expanded.

Nicheloa's eyes opened wide. He began to laugh. "I told you, Gaius, women do not understand our kind. She truly thinks you would give me up."

"By Gaius's own words, removing your head won't kill you," Agata said. "And I'll return it when I am done."

"You expect me to walk around without a head?" Nicheloa asked.

"I might take that one instead." She pointed at his pants. "You can live without that for a while."

The concubines sat straighter. They looked to the sky. Phillipa's face was neutral, but it felt as if she was smiling.

"You can't have my lictor's head," Gaius said. "Or his manhood."

"Then you're not worthy of the office you bear. I healed your servant with the power of my mind. I have turned this into a home with the power of my mind. You promised me you would do as I asked ... "

Gaius rose. He slapped her. "Take your place among the women, fourth concubine of Gaia, before I throw you into the sun."

Her ears rang and her cheekbone throbbed. "My name is Agata, and I am the wife of Jakub!"

He slapped her again.

"Take your place or go into the sun." He grabbed her shoulder. He cried out as the silver thread burned the pattern onto his right hand. Nicheloa and all the concubines gasped from the pain.

Gaius threw her to the ground.

Agata felt the wind knocked out of her lungs and a low burning in her right hand, but she smiled. The legend of silver was true. She might have her vengeance.

"I have no need for presumptuous women, and you

already said you don't want to be my concubine. Nicheloa, take her or destroy her as you please."

Agata ripped off the loosened sleeve of her silver threaded blouse. "I must regain my honor."

She jumped on Nicheloa's back and drew the sleeve against his throat as a garrote. She twisted the linen to ensure the thread was against his flesh, but it was the flesh of her throat which was burned by the silver. She screamed in agony as did Gaius who clutched his own throat. She dropped the garrote.

In her mind, Agata heard: *We won't help you take Nicheloa's head, but we would take this place from Gaius if we have an opening*.

Nicheloa pushed her to the floor. He drew a knife.

She looked up at his throat, though Nicheloa's flesh bubbled and was scorched and blackened, Gaius was still smooth. She touched her own throat. She did not feel blisters under her fingers.

"Wait," Gaius said.

"You said she was mine."

Pushing Nicheloa aside, Gaius grabbed her and lifted her to her feet. He punched her in the face.

"Lady Agata! Noooo ... " Ulpia's voice pleaded. "Don't hurt her!"

She felt blood squirt from her nose as she fell onto the floor. He kicked her in the stomach several times.

Through her bloody tears, there was a blur of movement as Ulpia jumped on Gaius's back. He grabbed the girl by the throat and threw her across the room. She screamed as she crumpled against the wall.

Titus ran to his daughter. His expression exposed the sorrow in his heart. She knew what it was to lose a child. Gathering Ulpia in his arms, he raced from the room.

"You said she was mine," Nicheloa said.

"And you were going to kill her so I changed my mind.

She is mine. Rape her with the knife before you kill her."

Nicheloa pressed his lips together and came towards Agata, knife in hand. His eyes showed he didn't like his task, but he learned long ago. Obey Gaius or die. "You brought this torture upon yourself."

Titus raced into the hall with an ax. Putting all his weight behind the blow, Titus struck Gaius in the back of the neck.

Holding the gash in his neck, Gaius arched his back and screamed. All the vampires shrieked with him. The concubines writhed on the floor. The sound echoed off the stone walls until it sounded like a thousand vampires cried. She shoved her hands over her ears, wounded by the noise. Agata couldn't breathe.

Titus lifted Agata to her feet. Agata's heart froze, then beat faster. She tried to protect her face from another blow. He pressed Nicheloa's dagger into her hand.

Confused by the action, but knowing she must act, she stabbed Nicheloa in the side of the neck. The pain echoed in her own body. She tried to remove the blade to cut his throat, but it stuck. She drew upward. It stuck again. The ballads never told her how hard it was to make a killing blow.

Titus handed her his ax.

With Nicheloa on his knees, Agata sliced his head from his shoulders. Blood spurted across her face, across her skirts.

The shrieks from her own mouth deafened her capacity to reason. Looking at the bloody dagger left in Nicheloa's neck and his severed head, Agata thought she might vomit. Gaius's furious scream pealed between his lips. It reverberated through every vampire. He held his own head as if he expected it to roll off his shoulders.

Blood pooled across the stone tiles.

Nicheloa's eyes were still open, moving. "Damn you,

woman. I knew I should have just killed you!"

"We will have no more of your cruelty, Legatus," Phillipa cried.

"You will take what I give you," Gaius screamed. "And … "

The concubines jumped on Gaius. The other two women's voices were screams of wild terror and fury. Only Phillipa's voice was more than a feral din: "For Jason!" and ripped Gaius's tunic. "For Claudia, For Laurel."

The women sweated blood as their hands ripped at his clothing and hair. Their nails ripped his skin. Phillipa kept screaming names. "For Paula. For Liliana … "

Gaius punched Sylvia. Her long curly head fell to the floor with a crack. Phillipa kept screaming names of former concubines.

Julia screamed as Gaius took her by the throat and threw her across the room. She jumped on the puddle and began to lick Nicheloa's spilled blood. Her wounds disappeared, and she grabbed on Gaius's head and exposed his throat.

"They were nothing; you're everything, Phillipa," Gaius screamed.

Phillipa ripped the dagger out of Nicheloa's neck. She stabbed Gaius in the throat. Agata could not move. Julia and Sylvia screeched, but Phillipa kept stabbing.

Gaius words were drowned by Phillipa's yell. "Come, Sisters!"

Agata followed the women as they chased him from the hall, down the stairs, and the fort. His screams evaporated, pursued by laughter. They gathered loose stones and threw them at Gauis.

Titus came up behind her. "Escape now, Honorable One. The vampire women did not win their freedom only to give it to you."

The three women turned towards Agata. Titus

stepped back as if he had not spoken.

"Do you think to rule us?" Phillipa asked.

"We had discussed it in depth long before you arrived. Phillipa will lead in Gaius's stead," Sylvia said, her fangs still exposed.

"As you will," Agata said.

"We can kill you without pain to ourselves," Sylvia whispered, taking a step towards her. "Do not think we were so foolish to underestimate you the way Gaius and Nicheloa did."

"Will you remain in fealty? Or go find your knight?" Phillipa asked.

"I must find Jakub."

"Then may your foolish love protect you." She kissed Agata's cheeks.

"May I take Nicheloa's head for Jakub, Lady Phillipa?"

"No. We must burn it along with his body," Julia said.

"If he reattaches his head, Nicheloa may yet take vengeance upon us. We cannot take the chance, Phillipa," Sylvia said. "Gaius must be kept at bay. His strength was his Lictor."

Agata could see the answer on Phillipa's face before she said, "Forgive us, Agata, but we must burn the body as the sun rises. You have fought beside us as a sister, so we will care for you during the execution and let you go in peace, but you have no claim upon anything within these walls."

The women were unnaturally quiet for victors in battle. Yet, Agata also did not feel like celebrating. There was nothing to celebrate. Men spoke of honor in battles, but all she saw was bloody butchery.

Titus smiled as he dumped straw and sticks in a pile into the fireplace furthest from the throne.

"Why are you helping us?" Agata said softly.

"Gaius said the words, but Nicheloa took what is

mine. And Ulpia will be safe from his lechery. He killed my other girls."

Sylvia and Phillipa dragged Nicheloa's body to the fireplace. Agata set down the head.

Julia handed Agata a torch.

Phillipa asked, "Do you want us to pray for you, brother?"

"Get it over with, you harpies," Nicheloa said. "I die happy knowing you'll suffer for your treason, you hag."

"I suffer happily knowing you'll die." Agata threw the torch onto his head. The hay caught quickly. Then his hair. The odor of burning flesh and greasy smoke filled the hall.

The other women set fire to his arms, torso, and feet.

Agata clenched her fists as his flesh smoked and blackened.

His skin blistered by the heat; she screamed and patted her own face. Over her cries of agony, Nicheloa shouted: "I knew you'd scream first."

Tears running down her face, she collapsed to the floor and clutched her knees to the chest.

Julia came beside Agata and embraced her.

Ulpia poured boiling tallow over Nicheloa's head and into his open mouth. He shrieked and sputtered then.

Agata curled into a ball, trying to drown the pain of being burned alive.

Sylvia set up the troughs, but Agata barely registered the mooing of another cow. She didn't hear its panicked bleats as it was slaughtered. She only knew it was dead when she tasted the precious irony blood that filled the cup, which Julia pressed against her lips.

*

Chapter 17

AT THE NEXT NIGHTFALL, TITUS AND ULPIA escorted Agata down the stairs of the fort. The walls of the Roman fort were still warm from the day's sun which grew stronger as the day's lengthened. Julia's garden plot held tiny seedlings which quivered in the mountain breeze. Further afield snowdrops had pushed through the frozen ground. It must be an omen of good tidings for the coven.

"What about you? Come with me," Agata asked.

"I'm bound to this place, Honorable One. Whether Gaius or Phillipa rule, they will eventually bring more children that someone must protect, but you're not bound to the fort. Your heart is bound to your knight. Find your home, and the Earth will protect you. Wrap it around you, so you might sleep."

"Thank you."

Though the night was beautiful, Agata feared the coming dawn. She perceived she might not make it in time. She must find shelter. She sought the tree she took protection in, but all the trees looked the same and none had a large opening.

A howl echoed through the cold night. Gaius wasn't dead. He was weakened, but he wasn't dead. He might follow her. She saw a wolf's shape in the darkness. *Could it be him?*

Agata ran as fast as she could. She found herself skipping over rocks, skidding down steep hills of gravel, bounding over boulders. Branches grasped upon her arms, ripped at her skirts. She ran faster, her sides felt they might split.

Her heart and lungs wanted to burst. Weakness overtook her muscles.

The sky lightened in the east. She sought a place to hide.

An eerie neigh rolled over the valley. *Oh my God, did Gaius have his horse? Weapons?*

She ducked behind a tree and peered behind her. She held her breath as Fideles and a rider in thick armor came closer.

"Hello, Sister," Sylvia said. She reached out her hand to Agata. "Come, Gaius has Nocte. Phillipa worried you might not make it home."

She pulled up Agata behind her.

"But the dawn?" Agata whispered.

"I know where Nicheloa hid from the dawn."

"Hid?"

Sylvia laughed. "A learned woman such as yourself must realize he had his hiding places. Some of the county seats are over a night's ride from our fort and he was leading livestock."

Seeing the obviousness of it, Agata laughed with her. The concubines were free. Agata was free, she had her vengeance, if not proof of it. What else was there to do except to go home?

*

Chapter 18

THE VAMPIRES EMERGED FROM THEIR HIDING place. Fideles knew the way to Râuflor without guidance from Sylvia or Agata. He had made the journey thousands of times over the long centuries.

Within hours, Agata saw the thick town walls, towers and familiar roof-line of her house against the herdlands. Her heart nearly burst from joy, but an icy feeling crept in her chest.

She had led Sylvia to the town where her children lived. A vampire anticipating freedom for as long as Phillipa would look for assurances that Agata would do nothing to harm them.

At the sacrificial herdland, Sylvia lowered Agata from Fideles back.

A single white ewe chewed grass. Was that the missing sacrificial sheep? Why was it here now?

"The treaty still stands between Phillipa and the counts?" Agata asked.

"The legend of the Legatus protects us all. I will return on the seventh day of the full moon as Nicheloa did before me," Sylvia said as she dismounted.

The ewe bleated in fear and bucked as Sylvia bit into its throat. Watching the other vampire watch her, Agata bit into the sheep's shoulder. She drank until its heart slowed. Sylvia and Agata left the rest for Fideles.

While the horse fed, Sylvia embraced her. "Let the

Gods blessings fall upon you, Sister," she said. You have several hours till the dawn. Use it well."

Agata crossed outside the city walls to the meadow near her home. In the darkness of night, she climbed the wall and slipped into the garden. Up close, the boards were gone. After only a week and a day, someone already lived there. She would discover who took her home after she rested.

Exhausted from her journey and satiated with sheep's blood, this time she did not fight the instinct to dig into a planted mound of soft, sweet Earth. Her nails and fingers moved the tilled soil easily.

The spicy, savory smell of her herbs surrounded her. She fell asleep, deep in the Earth, and knew sleep like she hadn't known since she had become a vampire.

*

AGATA UNLOCKED THE DOOR TO THE KITCHEN. She quietly moved through the house and ensured the other doors and windows were locked. Someone had been there. Hopefully, it was just Artur or perhaps Florin moving furniture or cleaning the pantry, but she wasn't sure. She wasn't even sure of the date. Only the sun had set and night had come.

She moved through the hallways. There were no signs of servants. Dust had settled in the corners. Items had been rearranged. She needed a priest to quarantine her in her house, but could not trust Bodgan, one of the church's other priest, or even the count's priest, Father Alexander.

Considering Titus's words, Agata returned to the garden. She filled an oil sack with Earth.

Through her bed chamber's window, she saw

movement on the upper floor. Could it be Gaius? Could he have followed her home? She did not sense him or any vampire nearby. She studied the form: Bogdan.

Fighting rage, she went inside. She placed the oilsack of Earth beside the bread oven and climbed the steps. She would see if human blood was as potent of medicine as the other vampires claimed.

At her chamber door, she said, “Have you made yourself comfortable, cousin?”

Bogdan screamed and held his cross in front of him. “This house belongs to me now, whore of a vampire. Bow before the power of God’s glory.”

“I do bow before God, but I don’t believe you’re his representative any longer, Ox. Plenty of men were forsaken in the Bible after they did not follow God’s law.” She ripped the cross out of Bogdan’s hands. She kissed it then gently set it upon her dressing table.

She pushed him onto the bed. “I followed every rule the Good Book claimed a woman must follow. Yet a feeble, cruel priest stole my house and my honor. You wanted Jakub’s wife,” Agata said smoothly. “Now I am what is left. With your last breaths, you will know me.”

Bogdan’s eyes brightened as she climbed on top of him.

Even though I threatened his death, he is aroused. He’s an idiot as well as an ox. Still, he is proof of the endurance of childhood pain. After I kill him, I must protect my children’s inheritance as well as I can.

Agata bit him in the femoral artery. A flood of human blood flew into her mouth.

Bogdan kicked when he realized she bit his leg. He tried to push her off; she bit down harder. Fangs expanded through her gums and latched onto his muscle. She drank in the salty lusciousness.

The rush of blood heightened her senses. Nothing she

had ever experienced compared to drinking the blood of one's enemy; she wanted to suck Bogdan dry.

He screamed. She wanted to make him scream again.

Agata craved for more than his death. She desired to eat his covetous eyes while he was still alive, then perhaps rip off each of his toes and fingers. She might listen to him beg for his life as she slowly took it.

No. She would have her vengeance, but she would not torture him. He was still Jakub's cousin.

His voice grew weak.

The flow of blood diminished. She searched his pale, sickly face for death.

"I ... " Bogdan gasped and tried to push her away. She was stronger.

"I won't turn you, but I have to kill you. Your hate of my husband might hurt my children someday." She kissed his lips and bit down, tearing at the flesh inside his mouth.

He gasped his last breath, sputtering saliva across her face. Agata continued to drink until his blood thickened, and his heart slowed. She felt the moment his heart stopped.

She had to plan. Someone knew where Bogdan was, and they would look for him eventually.

Let them believe he was a vampire too, perhaps not like Gaius, but a wretched thing.

Feeling stronger than she had since she changed, Agata carried Bogdan's body to the Kirchenburgen. It was silent this time of night.

She decided to place his corpse in the traditional method to kill a vampire. Count Mihai would be forced to claim Bogdan died a vampire. The populace would burn the body and drink the ashes.

She crossed herself. "God, forgive me. Judgment and vengeance are yours, but this man wronged me. I must protect my family."

Agata set the body in the pulpit. She pounded a nail into his forehead, put a stone in his open mouth, and hammered a wooden stake through his heart. She set a crucifix in his pants and left the hammer in his hand. Then she scrawled a note: I AM VAMPIRE.

She scribbled letters to her children and raced across town to Irina's home with an appeal to bring her fresh meat and blood once a week. She pressed the notes under the door and went home, satisfied in her night's work.

On her way, Agata tore the Mărţişors with silver tokens off the trees. Careful not to burn herself, she encircled the house and herb garden with the silver charms so she couldn't escape, but could still access her medicinal plants.

She wrote QUARANTINE DUE TO THE PLAGUE on a board and attached it to the front portcullis of her house. She took the silver thread from her best garments and blocked the portcullis and shuttered windows.

Agata would wall herself into her home. Even she ate nothing, but the flesh of rats, she would never hurt her family and neighbors. She was a lady of honor.

*

Autumn 1509

Chapter 19

WEAK FROM THE LACK OF FOOD, JAKUB'S stomach hadn't stopped rumbling for a day, but he needed his family more than sustenance. He should have rested Castor, but he wished to see Agata and his children: Artur and Daciana ought to be home at least. Perhaps, they could send word to Petru and Irina to come.

During his years away, Agata had written to him nearly every week. Then her letters stopped. He hadn't worried. Several times during the last offensive, he was delivered several messages at once. The battlefield, even his enemy, had shifted relentlessly. One day the letters would catch up to him—even if he was home first.

Once they were home, Castor could graze on fresh grass and herbs to his heart's content. After Jakub slept in his wife's embrace, he could visit with Irina and her new husband. It might be he was a grandfather. Agata would most likely be happy to be a grandmother; he wasn't sure if he was happy about being a grandfather. Even if his body ached with every morning, thirty-eight summers seemed too young.

From a distance, the house looked the same, but different. The herd and herdsman were not in the pasture. The stone road had grown mossy as if horses and carriages didn't come this way anymore. Agata's herb garden, which she had tended with such care, withered in places, and overgrew in others. No lights were cast from the windows.

Spiders had woven silver threads over the outer door. He saw the sign: QUARANTINE DUE TO PLAGUE.

His insides twisted. His training forced him to unburden Castor and let him graze.

After seeing so much death, if his wife and children had died from the plague, Jakub no longer cared about his fate. With the side of his fist, he pounded on the door. "Hello!" he cried. "Someone! Anyone! Hello!"

He heard someone shuffle inside.

"Agata? My lady? If you're there, you must let me in." He pounded on the door again. "I can hear you. Agata, is that you?"

"Jakub," his wife's sweet voice whispered. "Is that you?"

"Yes, let me in!"

Agata's gloved hand opened a window. Then she backed away from him.

Her apparition looked too pale for health, but she was not pockmarked, nor did he see any blackened gavocciolos or rotting flesh.

"I see no black death," Jakub said.

"I sent Daciana to be with Irina. Petru is doing well in his apprenticeship with Lexi, so he is there too. Artur is with Gravilla. I will die here but go see the children. Let them know I love them."

He pushed the wooden door with his shoulder. "Let me in! I have no life without you."

"Jakub, my love, if I will let you inside, you must cast me out and I will die."

"So you might die in the wilds? Never!" he said. "Let me in! I'm your husband. You must let me in."

The door creaked open.

Inside, the smell of furniture oil met him. Though no light shined due to all the closed windows, the furniture gleamed as if it had just been polished, and the rooms were clean. As he stepped into the darkness, lingering disappointment that he had come home to this, pressed in on him. *Why had I been on the battlefield if not to protect my family?* He could claim honor, and he served his Voivode well, but he had failed as a husband.

His wife's eyes wafted with bloody tears. "I have sent the servants away and moved into the kitchen, my love, but how I prayed I would look upon you again."

"I will not leave you until you make sense and tell me of your illness. Why do you cry blood?"

"I'm not contagious due to bad air. Only blood. I can prepare you a bath. See to Castor and I'll prepare it."

"I already have seen to my horse."

Agata boiled water in a pot. She took the rest of the water from her collection of rain barrels. Her hands trembled under the weight of the buckets, but she poured each one into the bath. Agata had always been industrious, but the work she did was beneath the lady's hands. It was work for a steward.

"Where are the servants?"

She threw rose petals, orange peels, and rosemary into the boiling water. He always loved that perfume. "I sent them away after I was attacked. I caught this infernal disease. I thought I was with child and now I'm this. Artur tried to protect me, but he was overcome by a stronger foe. Don't blame him. You mustn't blame him. How could any fourteen-year-old apprentice match a grown man with centuries of experience?"

Jacob had seen many raped. Common women, boys and girls who did not have knights to protect them.

I should've been here. Jakub didn't blame his son, he blamed himself. It was Jakub who had vowed to protect his wife.

"I no longer sleep well. I'm going mad. Did I tell you Petru and Daciana are with Irina? They are safer there.

Artur learns from his uncle's men."

"And the one who raped you?"

"I killed him. I think." She took the boiling pot and poured it into the tub of cooler water.

"What do you mean, you think?"

"I hoped I could show you his head like Chiomara, but I stabbed him in the neck and couldn't get the knife out. I took an ax to him. The other vampires threw him onto a pyre."

"You're a brave lady, Agata," Jakub said softly. "But vampires are legend. We used to laugh at peasants who believed in such things."

"We used to laugh at many things, but that doesn't make my fate any less true."

She stopped by the window and put her hand in the sun. Smoke wafted. He pulled her back inside.

"I don't think I have been forsaken by God. I can still do nearly everything I could before. But silver seems to cause a reaction and so does the sun. I'm writing a book about such things for Irina. No superstition, just medical fact."

Agata took a deep breath. "When you take another bride, see that she is kind to the children and industrious. That's how you'll know she'll make a fine wife."

Jakub didn't know what to say, he sputtered: "Take another bride?"

"I am of the walking dead, Jakub. My honor has been tarnished, and I have no proof I took vengeance. I have no hold on you."

Was God punishing me for what I have done while at war? It doesn't matter. Only Agata matters now. Jakub drew her close to him. ""You're my wife. I missed every deget of your face." Jakub kissed Agata's left cheek. Her brow. Her right cheek. He pressed his lips to hers.

"I've had other women: camp followers and

laundresses. But I've only wanted one wife. I've dreamed of you a thousand times. I will never leave you."

*

AGATA'S BODY REACTED TO HER HUSBAND AS IT always did, but this time, she had to focus to will her fangs to remain in her gums. She had missed him so much. All of her anxiety had come home. She could hear his heartbeat. She smelled his sweat. She ran her fingers through Jakub's straggly black hair which had grown to his mid back, tied with a simple ribbon. The lines on his brow had grown deeper, and his skin had grown darker from the sun, however, his chiseled cheekbones and the same nose he gave to Irina were still sculpted to perfection. His blue eyes which he gave to Irina and Petru had the same disquieting clarity as they always did.

He removed his clothing and stepped on a grated tray. A few new scars covered his body. She poured olive oil mixed with ash onto his shoulders. She scraped a strigil across his body to remove the dirt and excess oil.

He stepped into the warm rose bath. "Even though it will pain me, I want to know every detail of your adventure. Do not spare me, my love."

"I should air your clothes. Rest a moment and allow me to collect my thoughts."

Agata ran upstairs for his best embroidered cămaşa made linseed linen, sheepskin peiptar with the silver buttons, and white woolen pants decorated on the cuffs and pockets.

When she returned, tears burned her eyes. Yet, in a trembling voice, she told him everything.

Chapter 20

JAKUB STRODE ACROSS RÂUFLOR TO THE CASTLE. The ancient red bricks made way to creamy stone as the castle progressed toward the sky. Though he was a boy there, it was not his home. The house he built with Agata was his home. Behind him, the peasants whispered, he felt their eyes on his back. They feared him too much to speak openly. His brother's manservant opened the door. Gavrilla stood behind him.

"Welcome to my home, the brother of my husband," Gavrilla said, inclining her head. She did not meet his eye, but her fingers twisted around a handkerchief.

"I'm glad to see you are well, but was surprised to see my house in its present state."

Gavrilla eyes brimmed with tears. They were clear, just water.

"You miss her?" Jakub asked.

"Yes," Gavrilla said softly. "I miss her jokes. She was clever."

"Is clever."

Gavrilla met his eyes. "You won't have her put aside?"

"I love her."

"Thank you."

"You're not thanking God?" Jakub asked.

"I'll thank Him later. You answered my prayers. Come, my husband has much to say to you."

Gavrilla led them into the hall where his brother,

nephews, and eldest son sat. His old manservant, Florin, poured the wine. He wanted vengeance on existence. *How could life go on when Agata suffered?*

"Father, you've returned." Artur stood and inclined his head. He looked well, dressed in his uncle's livery, but his eyes betrayed his panic. "And Mother? Is she still unwell?"

Unwell? Unwell!

"Yes. I went to the house first," Jakub said, keeping his voice even. "And spoke to your sweet mother. Her concern for you, your brother, and sisters warmed my soul."

Mihai cleared his throat. "I might fear the voivode, but the Legatus of the Mountains is the true ruler of the county. He might burn Râuflor or our villages to the ground if he chooses or turn our children into slaves. Agata was a great lady, but she was lost as soon as he placed his eyes upon her."

Beside his uncle, Artur swigged a large gulp of wine.

Jakub wondered if Mihai would fear the Legatus as much if he knew he had been cast out of his fort by a group of angry concubines. However, Agata had warned, the vampire women would attack the county if their sacrifices didn't keep coming. It had been months. They might have retained men.

Jakub did not speak of the other vampires; instead, he studied his weakling brother who didn't protect his community while Jakub had ridden into battle in the name of Voivode Bogdan. The fur-lined coat didn't hide his soft muscles. His embroidered collars didn't cover his drooping doubled chin.

Jakub snapped, "You were to protect her!" .

"I ... " Artur started, but his uncle interrupted him.

"She was a great lady," Mihai repeated, "But she is just a woman. With the land long at war, there are plenty of young widows. Such sorrow is known to all men."

"You claim to know my sorrow. My children's sorrow?" Jakub slammed his cup to the table, sloshing the wine. Florin quickly wiped it up.

"Agata was destroyed, brother. While it pains you, put her aside," Mihai said. "I am supposed to see the voivode next month. Our house must be in order. No one of substance will admit the Legatus attacked her. All the counts surrounding the mountains claim the Legatus is peasant stories—even though we all offer him a goat or sheep every month."

"Then pray, why did he attack Agata and her cow?" Jakub asked.

"I don't know. Perhaps he wanted beef, rather than mutton. Or perhaps he wanted another woman," Mihai stated.

Jakub turned toward Artur. "And you, my son, do you claim your mother without honor?"

Artur looked between his father and uncle. "We were attacked. I could not protect her. She had honor once, but the priest claims her curse is bestowed upon God or my sword arm would not have failed."

His voice quivered. Artur did not believe his own words, but Jakub had no pity.

"How convenient for you," Jakub said. "Very well. I will protect this family from scandal, but I will go with her. And I pray your bride is never set upon as your mother was."

"You live too much on Chivalric tales, Father. Even Lucretia committed suicide," Artur said.

Jakub stood up. He buried his fingernails into his palm before his hand flew. Those were Mihai's words. No wonder Agata tried to regain her honor. Why Gavrilla feared what Jakub would do more than any curse from God.

"I was once proud of my son. May one day you live

to make me proud again, but I will not look upon the weakling boy who most likely would be dead if his mother hadn't also been in the barn."

"Father!" Artur cried.

"Your mother casts no blame. She has pride in her eldest son. I will never take it away from her, but I take no pride in a son who blames his mother for his failures.

"I will say goodbye to my other son and daughters. Then we will leave the county. Tell the Voivode whatever you wish. That Agata was attacked or she fell ill." He slammed down a written account. "This is Daciana's dowry. Irina is in charge of it.

"Artur, the house is yours. We will vacate it in a week."

*

IRINA'S HOME ON MERCHANT STREET WAS A FINE wooden house, beside her in-laws' older but equally fine house. She and Agata had done well with her marriage.

"Father!" Petru yelled from a window. "Irina, Father has returned!"

Irina quickly came to the door and welcomed him into her home. She kissed his cheeks, took his coat, and set a chair for him by the fire. Petru embraced him. However, Daciana clung to Lexi's leg as he brought a bench to sit beside him.

"This is your father, Cia," he said kindly. "Go, kiss him."

The child looked at Jakub disbelieving, not hiding her emotions. "My father is a knight!" she said. "Where's Mama? I want Mama!"

Jakub wasn't exactly surprised his youngest daughter did not know him, but it still hurt to see the little girl with Agata's eyes and black hair spurn him.

"I am a knight and your father," he said. "Your mother is still ill. She's at home."

"Where's your armor if you're a knight?" Daciana asked.

Lexi laughed. "Armor is only for battles, not visiting family."

Daciana pointed at the window.

"Where's Castor! Mama and Irina said you have a black warhorse with white socks named Castor. You walked here."

"It is a lovely day for a walk, sweetie. He is your father," Lexi said. "He has come home to set your house right."

Irina cringed but said nothing as she poured cups of spiced wine.

"When can I go home?" Daciana demanded.

"Not until Mama gets better," Petru said softly and took Jakub's hand. "I promise, Cia, this is our father."

Daciana let go of Lexi's leg. She hesitantly kissed Jakub's cheek and went back to Lexi's lap.

As much as he missed his elder children: the youngest didn't even know him. In truth, Jakub loved her, but he did not know her. She would not remember him. Agata had provided for the children's future as well as she could.

"Cia is healthy." Irina handed Jakub a cup of wine. "And happy. Petru is doing well in his apprenticeship."

"And are you happy?" Jakub asked Irina.

"Yes, Father. Lexi is a good man." She glanced at her husband. "I'm with child." She crossed herself to protect the baby inside her.

"As Agata informed me." To Lexi, Jakub said, "No doubt, you wish for a son?"

"Boy or girl, I only hope he is healthy and if God is good to us, he will look like Irina," Lexi said.

Jakub opened a leather bag. "Agata bade me bring

you these silver necklaces for you and this book of the truth about vampires. She has been conducting experiments upon herself. The ancient pact between the Legatus and the counties still holds, but if that changes, Agata wanted to give you and our descendants the knowledge to protect yourselves."

"You mean to go with her?" Irina asked.

"Yes. I have left Artur the house. You two will keep Daciana until she is of marriageable age?"

Lexi took Jakub's hand. "My dearest wife's father, as I promised Agata: Irina's sister is my sister. I will find her a good husband when she is of age. Agata gave me the instructions for both Petru and Cia."

"Good. I care less for a noble name; I want Daciana's husband to be kind and industrious. Being the granddaughter of two counts means little when both parents are not heirs. Find her a man with a good head on his shoulders. Irina, you will be training her in the healer's art when she is older?"

"Yes, Father," Irina said.

"Excellent. This bag has her dowry. I have left receipts with the count."

"We will find the best husband for her," Lexi said.

"And Mother?" Irina said.

"Your mother and I will be going away, so the scandal doesn't harm the county."

"Uncle Mihai means well," Petru said.

Jakub was annoyed Petru felt compelled to protect his uncle. He would not say any cruel words to his younger son. As Agata said, casting blame would only hurt his sons. After all, for much of their lives, their uncle had been home, while Jakub had been on the battlefield. Their uncle would provide for them after he was gone. He could not blame them, any more than Agata did.

He regretted his final words to Artur. "I'm sure

he believes he does. Let us not speak of scandals, but happy things. Petru, tell me all you have learned in your apprenticeship."

*

AGATA SMILED AS JAKUB LED A NEWLY purchased calf and hogget into the kitchen. She already had built salt trays to dry the calf meat and had spices mixed for sausages, but she felt a hollow sorrow. Everything was moving so fast.

"The children?"

"The children are well, my sweet wife," he said to Agata. "Daciana's dowry is safe. Petru is doing well in his apprenticeship. Gavrilla has found a match for Artur. Irina is happy and with child. We have been blessed."

"If you wish to leave me and stay with them, I will understand."

"You're worried about our children." Jakub kissed the top of her head. "Irina is married. Artur is grown. Petru has begun his apprenticeship. No little sister has ever been so loved as Cia.

"Still, I will regret leaving our children behind. I realized how much I did not know them. We are bound by blood, but we are strangers."

Her heart ached. She had prayed for Jakub to return from war and he had come home. She knew she must leave Râuflor, but if he went with her, he would be separated from the children once more.

"The vampires told me losing our children and grandchildren to eternity would cause us great pain. I would spare you from this pain if I can."

"You cannot spare me from anything," Jakub said. "I have done cruel things, profane things. Heaven has no place for me if you're not there. Like all men, I've had other women, but only one wife. I will become like you, and we will leave Râuflor."

"Do you think we must leave immediately? Before Irina has her baby?"

"Listen well. We cannot stay here. Râuflor would eventually tire of living beside two vampires," he said. "And then our children will truly be in danger."

Agata lifted her chin to look at her husband. Her lips quivered, but she knew he was correct. She finally admitted the truth, which she hadn't wanted to face. That Sylvia Phillipa, Nicheloa, and Gaius warned her about. "I thought if I regained my honor, we could be a family again, but our existence won't ever be the same, will it?"

"No, it won't be," Jakub said. "Eternity will leave us with plenty of time to regret. Now we must think and plan. I will need your mind as you need my experience. You won't make our children pay for any folly of their parents. You're too kind of a mother. Now tell me how to travel under the sun?"

"What about your leather coat?" Agata said. "Over linen and wool, leather surely would block the sun."

"Indeed, my love."

"I could hide under coats for now. Where was it you wanted to go, my husband?"

"The Franks." Jakub's eyes seemed to glow with an inner light.

"Why to the Franks?"

"Because their knights believe in chivalry though they currently have a king called the Father of People. They are noble and kind. The language is similar to our own, but we must practice," Jakub said. "And, perhaps I can become landed by great deeds. We can start again. Though it pains me, you will need to sell off many of your treasures to finance this venture."

"You are my only treasure." Agata kissed her husband's lips.

*

Chapter 21

After their errands in Râuflor were complete, Jakub drove the horse and cart south along the main road to Bodești which edged the eastern side of the Carpathian Mountains. A long journey was in front of them on roads of questionable quality with an even more dubious map to the Black Sea. There, they would acquire passage on a ship to take them to the land of the Franks. He wasn't sure if he should go through the Principality of Wallachia or head north-west following the foothills which might be covered in snow. He feared crossing into the Ottoman Empire with his wife.

One horse easily pulled the small cart on narrow mountain roads. His warhorse, Castor, was tethered behind the wagon. Behind Castor was a freshly shorn yearling hogget for Jakub's transformation. The deep forest of spiraling and twisted pines cast the road in dappled golden shade. The canvas tent was lined with leather and tapestries to protect them from the sun and the rain. Agata was safe inside with oil sacks of earth from her garden. Besides, insulation, the tapestries they were light-weight and precious, hopefully, valuable enough to hire a ship.

Every hour, he found himself going over Agata's list again in his head. He wanted everything to go perfectly. If he was a younger man without a hint of gray in his black locks, he might have waited to arrive in France or at least a port city for the transformation, but the life of a soldier was a hard one. He did not want his body to age another night. Unless they turned around, the children—and the rest of the village—would be safe.

As the sun lowered, he came to a shallow creek. "We'll make camp here."

"Yes, my love," Agata said through the canvas.

Jakub pulled off the road into a somewhat smooth and level ground. He jumped down from the cart to unhook and hobble the horses. His boots slipped under soft wet earth broken up by patches of grass. He watched the bugs skimmed lazily over it. Day birds quieted, and nightbirds and bats ruled the canopy of trees overhead.

His last sunset.

At dusk, Agata emerged. As he helped her down, he noticed in the cart, she had spread rose petals and wolfsbane between their blankets where they made love. She opened her can of smoldering torchwood and let the sparks fall onto a few pieces of wood and moss. Her work was efficient as always.

"I am reminded of so many years ago when we left our bridal bed and ran out to the herdlands to make love under the stars," he said, watching as she poked sausages with sticks to hang over the fire.

"And we were caught by the servants," Agata said with a girlish giggle.

"Mihai was so angry. He was so worried we'd cause a scandal."

Agata smiled at him. "We did."

*

LYING BESIDE HER HUSBAND, AGATA LISTENED to his rhythmic heartbeat and soft sounds of his body digesting his dinner. He ran his fingers down the smooth skin of her inner arm. She whispered, "Are you ready?"

"Yes."

"I will love you for eternity," she said.

Staring deep into his eyes, she lifted his wrist to her lips. She bit into it and sucked the blood from the wound.

He groaned as his heart fluttered. She bit open her own wrist and pressed it to his lips until he calmed.

Agata sliced open the flesh over his heart. He screamed loudly when she expanded her fangs and bit down, gulping the blood which poured into her mouth. His heart slowed. She listened for the moment his pulse shuddered.

She opened her breast and pressed his head to the wound. There was no hesitation as he swallowed her blood to be reborn into undeath.

Agata felt the infinity of the line of vampires into which she and Jakub were resurrected. Nicheloa. Gaius. A beautiful African woman. A tall man who stood in shadow. A hideous hunchback. A lad no older than Artur. All these souls and others were linked through blood.

She did not remember seeing these people during her change and wondered if Jakub could see them the way she did. The line of vampires disappeared as a hot rage overtook her vision. It was as if Gaius sensed Jakub and turned his eyes towards them. He would come for them. He desired revenge for what she had done.

Feeling the danger which Gaius posed, she wanted to flee with her husband, but his lips still sucked on her flesh, consuming her blood. She had no idea how much he needed to become a vampire, but if they stopped now, he might die.

All around them, the forest was full of deer and rabbits and insects buzzing, but she sensed no vampires. She said a quick prayer for God's guidance and protection and thanked Him for the bounty which they would consume.

Jakub fell to his back, clutching his left arm and

pressing it to his chest. She could not shield him from the pain of death.

Agata silently moved into the glen where the hogget chewed on hay. After she tethered the hogget's legs, she opened the sheep's throat. She smiled as the blood streamed into a deep pan. The red liquid piqued her thirst, but she willed herself to remain in control.

Jakub shouted as he awoke from death.

"I am here, my love." She carried the pan to where he lie.

Using small wooden cups, they both feasted on the blood. They slurped and gulped the sheep's vital fluid like wine until their thirst slackened. Jakub licked the pan, not willing to waste a drop.

Jakub's stomach growled loudly. "There were days spent in battle where I didn't touch a morsel, yet I never remember a hunger such as this."

"It's our need for blood. It makes us hungrier. Take the heart."

With his knife, he cut out the sheep's heart. He plunged his teeth into the bloody muscle.

Not willing to waste the carcass, she carved the flesh into steaks, rounds, and other pieces.

Still hungry, like the newly reborn monster he was, Jakub picked up the scraps and sucked the marrow from the bones. The meat was packed in an oilcloth before Jakub had his fill.

As if he were drunk or in a daze, Jakub stumbled to the creek and let the water spill over his body.

With oil soap, Agata joined him in the icy water. They washed each other before climbing into the wagon for the coming day.

Agata let down her coil and let her raven hair tickle Jakub's chest as she cuddled to him. Finally, willing to speak of her fear, she whispered, "When I transformed you, did you see him, Gaius? The Legatus of the Mountains?"

"Yes, I saw him."

"He wants vengeance."

"Yes." He ran his fingers down her spine. "If I remember my war history, Gaius Lepidus Severus was a great general who won many wars until one day he disappeared. Great generals aren't known for taking their losses lightly – especially from a smaller foe he underestimated."

"I would fear the sun if not for the cart, but perhaps we ought to sell it and tapestries? If I had my own leathers, we could travel twice as fast," she asked.

He kissed her brow. "I would think the sanctuary from the sun is more important than speed. Moreover, the cart carries the earth from your garden. Even if Gaius knows where we camp tonight, he doesn't know which way we travel."

Agata nodded.

"I'm here now; there's nothing to fear."

Agata nodded again and squeezed his hand, but she was afraid.

His chest rose and fell with a sigh. "So, this is the life of a monster? It's not quite what I expected if I'm honest."

THE END

IF YOU ENJOYED THIS BOOK, PLEASE LEAVE A review at your favorite book site or simply tell all your friends!

*

AND THERE ARE MANY OTHER VAMPIRES WHOSE stories are told in the Paper Flower Consortium. I hope you enjoy:

Chivalry Among Vampires

Paper Flower Consortium Podcast

Norma's Cleaning Service Mysteries
Death Pulls a Stake Out
Death Hears a Siren
Death Sticks a Pixie

Immortal House: A Nightmarish Tale of Vampires and Real Estate

And more to come...

ABOUT THE AUTHOR

MUCH TO HER CHAGRIN, ELIZABETH GUIZZETTI discovered she was not a cyborg and growing up to be an otter would be impractical, so began writing stories at age twelve. Three decades later, Guizzetti is an illustrator and author best known for her demon-poodle based comedy, ***Out for Souls & Cookies.*** She is also the creator of ***For the Love of Pancakes***, ***Faminelands*** and ***Lure*** and collaborated with authors on several projects including ***A is for Apex*** and ***The Prince of Artemis V***.

To explore a different aspect of her creativity, she writes science fiction and fantasy. Her debut novel, ***Other Systems***, was a 2015 Finalist for the Canopus Award for excellence in Interstellar Fiction. Her short work has appeared in anthologies such as ***Wee Folk and The Wise*** and ***Beyond the Hedge***. Other credits include: I*mmortal House, The Grove Chronicles of the Martlet, and The Light Side of the Moon.*

Guizzetti lives in Seattle with her husband. When not writing or illustrating, she loves hiking and birdwatching.

To find out more about her work follow her on Twitter @E_Guizzetti

Other Titles

Comics

Faminelands
Out For Souls & Cookies!
Lure
For the Love of Pancakes

Novels and Novellas

Other Systems
The Light Side of the Moon
The Grove

Chronicles of the Martlet
The War Ender's Apprentice: Book 1
The Morality of a Necromancer: Book 2
The Assassin's Twisted Path: Book 3

Illustration Projects

A is for Apex written by Jennifer Brozek
The Prince of Artemis V written by Jennifer Brozek

www.ingramcontent.com/pod-product-compliance
Lightning Source LLC
Chambersburg PA
CBHW070502170726
48291CB00008B/2616

* 9 7 8 1 9 5 0 7 0 8 0 6 2 *